Crone Wisdom

Sarah Lewin

Published by Sarah Lewin, 2023.

CRONE WISDOM

First edition. October 6, 2023.

Written by Sarah Lewin.

To my four beautiful children - Peter, Anita, Emma and Katharine, you are my motivation and my reason for always striving to do my best.

I was born with a love of books and I have always loved reading and writing about the world around me. I am fascinated with the magical world of imagination and what if. I am a passionate writer and I like to think that I use words to ignite imagination. As a mother and teacher, I love writing for children. As I grow older, I have rediscovered a love of magic, fairies and witches. As well as writing children's books and books about magic in the everyday, I publish a monthly column in the local paper – tips and ideas for everyday health and wellness, mind, body and spirit. You can also read my weekly blog at sarahlewin.com or follow me on Facebook. When I am not reading or writing you will probably find me in my garden at home. Herbs, flowers, fruits and vegetables, I am always creating magical spaces for birds, insects and the local wildlife. Occasionally I run workshops, sharing what I am passionate about, because it is fun to share with others. I hope you enjoy my books and I welcome all questions, and feedback on my writing.

This book, my first novel, is dedicated to my four children – Peter, Anita, Emma and Katharine. They have taught me so much about being a mother, being a human, about love and forgiveness and I love them all "bigger than the sky."

Crone Wisdom
Sarah Lewin

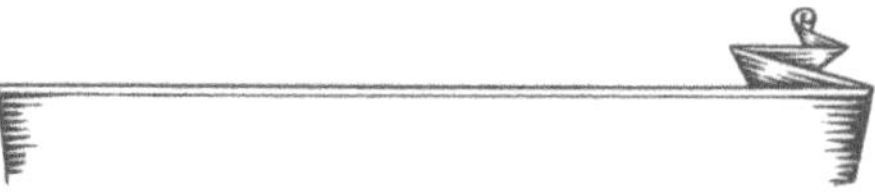

Introduction - The Wisdom of the Crone

With age comes wisdom, and an awakening of a sense of self from years ago and from previous lifetimes.

The wizened crone eyed the huge, shiny red apple. She wondered, if like herself, the outer skin of the delicious-looking fruit belied what lay beneath. Glancing in the mirror, the crone startled, still surprised by the aged face full of wrinkles that stared back. Her long, flowing grey hair drove her crazy, but she refused to cut it. Instead, every morning she wound it up into a bun, high up on the top of her head. Her grey-green eyes, her mother's eyes, stared back at her. She remembered a lifetime ago being cranky that she had her mother's eyes when instead, she wished for the piercing blue eyes of her father. Her face had the normal wrinkles and crow's feet under her eyes. Her nose, huge, like any other witch. Whilst never called a beauty, she guessed she was not the ugliest woman in the world, even by today's materialistic standards.

She would not necessarily change her appearance, given the choice. The wisdom that comes with age beyond years was too valuable to lose. Of course, having the understanding and knowledge of the way of the witch and the way of the world would have been handy years ago. As with all magical gifts, sacrifice is often the key. Losing her children and gaining knowledge was a crap way of becoming a magical, mythical creature. She would have preferred a lifetime watching her children grow up. To teach and guide them in the ways of the world. Why could fate not have gifted her both with many years of family, followed by many more years of magic? She sighed, knowing that this was not the way of things.

Laying the apple back in the wooden crate she had shaped from the willow tree saplings growing around her cottage, she picked up her quill. Dipping the tip into the ink well filled with spinach berry juice, she began her *Book of Spells*.

Every good guidebook starts at the beginning. Normally with a paragraph or two about the key thing for the reader to learn. The crone began her *Book of Spells* with an explanation of how the changes in the seasons influence behaviour. This was the one most significant piece of knowledge that she had learnt along her journey. The way the changes in seasons and cycles affect our thoughts and actions. Even after many years of practising the craft, she was still learning. She felt an enormous obligation to write down what she had learnt for future generations.

Whether mystical or mundane normal folk, the correspondences of the seasons and cycles, celebrations, harvest and worship were undeniably linked to nature. In the magical world, this was known as the witch wheel, containing eight key sabbats, or celebrations throughout the normal calendar year. These celebrations occurred at key points in the earth's natural calendar during times of seasonal significance. Whilst not linked to the moon phases, the phases of the moon played a significant role in the story of magic folk worship.

These significant days are not man-made, nor do they commemorate any specific historical event. Neither are they randomly chosen days like Mother's Day. The eight sabbats of witchcraft are not man-made because they existed before man. They are as old as the earth itself, the essence of nature. The earth, its orbit around the sun, the moon, the stars, it is all aligned.

Once a year, there is a longest night and a shortest day, the winter solstice or Yule. There is also a shortest night and the longest day, the summer solstice or Litha. The dates for these events depend on the hemisphere we live in.

She smiled.

IT ALL MADE SO MUCH more sense now than at the beginning. These days, the ebb and flow of nature was as much a part of her as breathing or walking. The other two witchy celebrations, as old as the earth itself, the spring equinox, Ostara, and the autumn equinox, Mabon: the days when day and night were both of equal length. Drawing it all in her book gave Luna a great sense of satisfaction. As if now she was really a magical creature who cast spells, danced in the moonlight, and made potions for love and wealth. She felt humbled to be honouring the goddess and spirits during these days and the celebrations of Imbolc, Beltane, Lammas and Samhain.

The crone, was she fifty-five years old, sixty-five years old or over a hundred years old? She found it difficult to remember. Having travelled across worlds so many times across the last thirty years, she was no longer sure. She remembered with absolute clarity some of her lives, past lives and present. She had known devastation, loss, tragedy and absolute joy. She had learnt the art of letting go, of celebrating and being happy because she was alive. Life's lessons had been tough, but she tried to remember there was always something to celebrate.

In Australia, Litha, the summer solstice, midsummer, the longest day of the year, was celebrated just before Christmas. The old crone loved dancing around the bonfire, making crowns out of daisy chains. The daisy chains she made today linked her with the daisy chains made with others, such a long time ago. Her kitten, Salem sat up as she casually flung a tiny daisy crown over his head. He was used to the crone's way of dancing and flowers and all things witchy. He, too, was blessed that the old crone had found him in the back garden at a time when they needed each other.

Luna paused, right in the middle of a twirl, remembering the time of year. She swept up her little kitten and his daisy crown and cuddled him tight.

If only midsummer wasn't the same week as Christmas. Despite Christmas being an essentially pagan celebration, this witch never ever acknowledged that particular day, ever.

Maiden, Mother, Crone
What I know now, I never could have known
How cruel and unfair, we can not change the past
But let's make today last as long as we can
And dream of a tomorrow where all our dreams come true
Mending bridges, healing hands,
Stretching out across the lands to one and all
A mother's call
So mote it be

The Christmas Curse

People come into our lives for a reason. Sometimes they stay, sometimes they move on.

Luna

The crone stood up from her old worn, patchwork chair, its seat faded after many years of use, her joints creaking as she stretched, her fingertips touching the wooden beams on the ceiling of her ancient cottage. Hobbling to the door, she grabbed her green corduroy gardening apron, slinging it over her shoulder. It was heavy and large and the perfect size to hold all the tools she needed in her garden. Outside, she squinted at the sun gleaming off the neighbour's solar panels. She fumbled in her apron for sunglasses. Reluctantly putting them on, she muttered, "There are some perks of being an ancient witch in a modern world."

Salem stretched his tiny black furry feline body, uncurling from his favourite sunny spot just outside the purple door. Just to the right of the welcome mat, out of the way of the door when it opened. He wound his way through his mistress's feet, taking care not to trip her up.

Luna bent down to pat Salem, changed her mind, and scooped him up, depositing him in one of the large pockets of her apron. She loved him to bits. Her little black stray that she had found in the back garden, lost and forlorn. They had quickly formed a bond of friendship and love. At a particularly tough December date, Salem had arrived to remind Luna that she was loved and lovable.

Her whole life she found relationships with fellow humans confusing, frustrating, and disappointing. Starting with her strictly religious parents, to whom she was a disappointment, to her bully of a husband, even her children, whisked away far too soon.

Cats were delightfully uncomplicated. Loving yet independent, playful and serious, cats were marvellous.

Out of the corner of her eye, she saw Maude the Magpie fly past, settling on the perch nearby. The crone had made the perch for her feathered friend after one of her eucalypt trees had lost a branch in a storm. Hating to throw anything useful away, she had fashioned it into a perch attached to the other large tree just near the front door.

"Hello, my friend," the crone crooned as she tossed a handful of seed Maude's way.

She knew magpies generally preferred meat, but this witch was not buying meat or meat products for anyone, not even her beloved animal family. Salem was the only exception. She had relented, providing him with a concoction including fish, mainly tuna, which she sourced during her monthly shop in the village.

"Time for healing," whispered this maiden, mother, crone, kneeling down, placing her hands in the soft earth, gentling tidying the weeds and herbs entwined together. The rich black soil she had created with her own mix of newspaper, food scraps, plant waste and soil from the garden. It crumbled in her hands, running between her fingers. Not too much clay, nor too much sand. It didn't dry out too quickly, which saved on watering.

"It may have taken me years to create this mix, but it is far better than I ever could have imagined. If only I could heal the perpetual generational trauma curse as easily," Luna always spoke to her plants. The roses, lavender, rosemary and peppermint were like her children.

"Such a curse is not as easy to heal, not even by spell work. Some curses, the kinds that have been twisted and turned around, entwining families for generations, can take generations to unravel and heal. Like these weeds that keep coming back, no matter how many hours I spend in this garden."

LUNA HAD LEARNT MANY things as she studied the way of the witch. Time, effort, patience, gratitude and never giving up. She was blessed to have found her little cottage. Blessed to be able to tend to her herbs and flowers in the cottage garden on the edge of town, somewhere in outback Australia, in 2023.

Stella

Stella, a nearly forty-year-old, single mum of four, was alone in the house. It was the kids' weekend with their father. During this time, when the house was so very quiet, she had taken to talking to herself. She found it cathartic to rant and rave and say what she would never say to anyone else.

"I know it sounds melodramatic, but I seriously do wonder if I am cursed. Not just at Christmas time, but a generational curse that passes through generations on Mum's side of the family. Catching sight of her reflection, breathing a sigh of relief that her hair had not yet turned grey.

"As far back as I can remember, every school holiday, and each Christmas, I would spend all day sitting still, reading books, writing stories, doing jigsaws or playing solitaire." After the holidays, schoolmates would tell her tales of spending time running wild with cousins, at the beach, at grandma's or by the river.

"It's not my fault all my grandparents had passed before I was born," Stella said, stabbing the pen on the paper where she was supposed to be writing her to-do list.

"I know my grandmother's spirit often stood at the foot of my bed when I was very small, watching me."

Growing up, Stella had no idea she was part of a big family, with a multitude of cousins, both maternal and paternal. Her mother would never speak about family or the past. It was only when she found the old sepia photographs one day, snooping in the office cupboard.

"I would like to lift this curse, not so much for me, as for my children. I want their lives to be happy, healthy, full of love, laughter, peace, joy and abundance." Stella raised her eyes to the heavens. "I call on my guardian angels and spirit guides who have looked after me, to hear my plea and lift this curse."

STELLA DIDN'T DISAGREE with the theory that many of her issues may well have stemmed from losing her dad six weeks before she turned ten years old. Not so much because she had Daddy issues, but because existence in the family home after his passing was so very sad and lonely.

"I still remember he was supposed to teach me judo when I reached double figures. That was definitely a turning point in my life. I don't remember much else about being little. I don't remember laughing or having fun. I know I loved reading and that I spent a lot of time quietly lost in the world of Enid Blyton or the Lion, the Witch and the Wardrobe."

Peeking through the curtains at the neighbour's pool, her eyes watered as she remembered more about so long ago.

"Dad loved taking us to play in the pool. Mum must have hated it, but she did keep the pool clean, so we could use it, at least until I had left home."

"I guess apart from Dad, the one other thing I miss from my childhood is my cat."

A cat lover from an early age, Stella remembered fondly paying fifty cents for a part Persian kitten at the school fete. Her mother was horrified and mortified, and tried to give it back. Grudgingly though, she had been allowed to keep Whiskers.

When she wasn't reading, Stella and Whiskers spent many hours in the garden. Her mother had let her have a patch of garden amongst the manicured grass, the roses, geraniums, azaleas and gardenias. Spending her pocket money on pansies and petunias, keeping the playful kitten away from the fairies living in the petals until he was old enough to understand they were friends.

Remembering how her mother held herself, how she refused any offers of help or friendship, she was convinced the curse ran deep, traversing and entwined over many generations and lifetimes.

"I know I remember a couple of my past lives. I was a witch in a coven with other women. We probably only read books, played in the garden, danced during the moon and had cups of coffee together." Stella danced a little waltz around the clean and tidy living area with her lime green feather duster held like a magic wand.

"I remember being powerful and bossing people around. For real, not just in a dream, or was it a dream?" Stella wondered. She also remembered being a gypsy. Complete with an old colourful caravan full of herbs and medicine bottles and potions and lotions.

Outspoken and influential or poor, she had a feeling that in each of her past lives, she had ruffled feathers. Intentionally or unintentionally, she made people uncomfortable.

"I am sure that I made people so enraged that they threatened to curse me, and did curse me." Striking a pose of authority, she stood on her tiptoes in her cabled knitted Ugg boots, her purple daggy tracksuit pants and her pink flannelette shirt. She couldn't help giggling at her pose. Then suddenly serious again. "I also think someone on Mum's side of the family made someone jealous and we got cursed there, too!" With a flourish, she flung the duster and nearly tripped over the cord of the vacuum cleaner.

Moving to the large linen cupboard at the front of the living area, she took out the big box with the family photo album. It was an old-fashioned album, one with sticky pages. Once those photos were put in, they were stuck there for life. She had found it when she cleaned out the cupboards after her mother passed onto the next life.

"Mum certainly surprised me. But then she always was organised." She had found not one but two family albums. Complete with exactly the same photographs and identical notes. "One for each of us." Stella and her sister had never been close. She had only spoken to her on the telephone on birthdays and Christmas since Mum died five years ago.

She read through the notes scribbled next to the sepia photos, some taken nearly one hundred years ago.

Although she didn't know much about her family, there were some things she knew.

For example, her Dad and his family were all staunch Catholics. Outspoken, one-eyed Catholics. They had suffered greatly during World War II and their experiences in the aftermath of the war.

"I do understand why they were outspoken and thought they were right. Part of that seems to be a generational thing. Not necessarily just Catholics." Stella remembered the couple of times she did meet some of Dad's family. The night before his funeral. At the age of nine. When she was asked to play guitar for her Dad's sisters. Strangers, grieving for their brother, her Dad.

There was no doubt that her father's family had done it tough. He and his seven siblings were born before World War II. Looking at the photos of her grandfather, a NSW policeman, she remembered the stories of living in different regional locations in NSW. Her dad had gone to school in Orange, Bega and Cowra. Stella's aunts had become a doctor, a teacher, a farmer, all strong women, all independent and yet fiercely loyal.

Stella looked at the photo of her dad, wearing a Scottish kilt and uniform. At seventeen, he signed up to the Royal Australian Air Force, becoming a Morse code operator on a ship off the coast of New Guinea during World War II. He lied about his age, stating he was eighteen.

"I still have his hat somewhere. I still have no idea why he was in the Scottish regiment."

Stella remembered being told that her dad had caught malaria in the jungles of New Guinea, or on the ship off New Guinea. Sometimes at home, he would have to go and lie down in the dark and the quiet because he suffered migraines, fever, chills, muscle aches and pain many years after returning home.

Back from the war, he put himself through university to become a dentist by driving cabs in Sydney at night. Stella gazed at the photo of herself and her dad in a park in Sydney.

"The best holidays ever. Driving to Sydney in the school holidays. Feeding the pigeons at Hyde Park, across from the hotel, and going shopping at David Jones." She smiled, remembering how posh she used to think those trips were.

In contrast, Stella's mother's family was all Church of England. In her mother's family were actresses, dancers, artistic types.

"I am so glad that as an adult, I got to meet some of my cousins. They were all so friendly and down to earth." They had shared some family stories with her, welcoming her with none of the religious prejudices of the previous generation.

Sometimes when Stella looked at the photos, she was sure she had met her ancestors.

"They seem so familiar, as if I know them. But all my grandparents had died before I was even born." A fact that always bought tears to her eyes.

"I did love spending time with my cousins on Mum's side. Even if it was only a couple of hours on Boxing Day every other year. It seems like such a long time ago. A whole other life," Stella mused.

"DOES STRESS AND TRAUMA play tricks with memory?" Stella was sometimes concerned that she drank too much alcohol. She drank to block the pain of losing her kids, to block emotions altogether.

"I do have to try to drink less alcohol. And coffee. I get too jittery. Although maybe I am jittery anyway."

She eyed the cask of wine in the fridge as she reached for the milk.

"Coffee now. Green tea later," she promised herself. "And I really must stop drinking wine from my coffee mug. I seem to be going through casks more quickly than I used to." Stella wasn't good with self-control.

The other odd thing, and she wasn't sure whether it was linked to her alcohol consumption, was really weird dreams.

"I have never remembered my dreams before." She sat at the kitchen bench, something she had started doing when her kids weren't there. She felt close to them, sitting where they had sat for breakfast, lunch and dinner. She eyed the notebook under the white fruit bowl.

"I must clean that out. Those bananas need making into bread." She wrinkled her nose at the smell of fruit part its best-use date. She lifted the notebook out and grabbed a pen from the fruit bowl.

"What was last night? I remember a cliff, a full moon, and some women chanting." Stella wrote down all the details she could remember. "I am sure there was more." She looked around the kitchen as if for inspiration. "Ah, that's right! That school room, and the long corridor." Her dreams were blurry like there was a veil between herself and the action.

Was she simply remembering scenes from movies or books she had read?

"Sometimes it feels like I am back at home, but the secret door takes me somewhere different. There is a long covered verandah, and school room. It feels like home.

"I bet it is just part of a scene from a book I read when I was little."

Getting restless, Stella walked to the desk where she still had the album open. She loved the black and white photo of her parents' wedding. "It's easy to tell Mum was older than her brother and sister. Seventeen years older is a lot though." She still had photos of her mum's father, one of the pilots who set world records in planes between England and Australia during the time of Sir Kingsford Smith.

Stella flicked through to the end of the photos just before her dad passed away.

"No wonder I was called the snob on the hill. They both looked so elegant and posh, dressed up for their dinner parties. Being friends with other dentists, doctors and even solicitors." She tried to remember those times when she sat with the babysitter while Mum and Dad partied. "I think I remember some of their friends. Or maybe I dreamt that part too." After her dad died, her mum sat home, at the dining table overlooking the town, doing crosswords or sewing and maybe creating cross stitch.

There were also photos of the garden.

"Mum did love her garden, especially the azaleas, geraniums, roses, hydrangeas and whatever those native bushes were." Stella remembered hiding in the terraced garden, talking to her imaginary friends, the fairies and elves.

"And painting, and the art galleries." Stella used to go with her mum and her friends when they established the local art galleries. One of the galleries had been in the back rooms at home, so her mum would be home before and after school.

Strong women on both sides of the family.

Stella slammed the album shut, shoved it back into the box and put the box right in the back of the cupboard.

"That's it!" she said, stamping her feet like a spoiled child.

"I will break the curse!" Stella had been determined not to repeat the mistakes of her parents when she married and became a mum to four beautiful children. She discovered that unfortunately, history has a way of repeating itself.

"I was sure I could be a better parent than mine were. I would be much more attuned to my kids, their feelings and needs. How was I supposed to know that it wasn't going to work out!" She shouted to the empty room.

"How come the days are longer when the kids aren't here?" Stella wondered. "Is it too early for a wine yet?"

"No wine today," the tiniest whisper.

Stella shook her head as if clearing her ears. As she opened the fridge to reach for the cask, she again heard, "Not today." Such a tiny voice.

"I must be going mad!" She looked around, but of course there was no one there.

Stella took her cup of tea and sat outside, watching the full moon rise above the distant hills. The sky had a strange purply-red tinge she hadn't seen before. A green frog jumped up onto the table next to her.

"I know I don't have confidence in my ability as a parent, as a mother," she told the amphibian. "I doubt myself ALL the time. Everyone else seems to be better at everything, I get it all wrong." Froggy seemed to be listening, staring intently at the young mother.

"That I know that I did the best I could with the knowledge and experience available to me at the time is of little comfort."

"How on earth can I parent Pedro, Kay, Emily and Andie when their dad and his family have such different ways of parenting? They have such different views on everything," she told her new friend.

"I guess now, it has been five years, Pedro and Kay are out on their own, and Emily and Andie are nearly adults. Is it time to stop beating myself up for failing at being their mother?"

Out of the corner of her eye, she saw something move in the shadows. She stared, wishing she had her glasses on, but she couldn't make it out. The leaves in the hedge at the bottom of the garden rustled.

"What on earth was that?" she asked. The frog jumped off in the other direction.

"Did that noise scare you too Mr Froggy?" Stella leant over, trying to find where her new friend had disappeared to.

"Do I go and see what that noise was?" she wondered. She decided against it. It was dark down in that corner of the garden.

"I guess it is bedtime. Goodnight Mr Frog, wherever you are." Stella locked the back door behind her.

Snuggling under the blanket, without having had any alcohol, she thought it would be difficult to fall asleep. She always started by saying goodnight to each of her children, being grateful for the time she spent with them.

The next thing she knew, she was standing in a field where there was a big bonfire burning. There were figures in black robes dancing around the fire. The full moon in the sky looked the same as the one in her backyard.

"I guess it is," she thought.

She concentrated on the scene in front of her. She could hear the chanting.

"Let go of the fear, don't let the bullies get you."

"Be confident, you can do this!"

"Love yourself and accept yourself first!"

"You are good enough. Maiden, mother, crone."

"Family, children, parenting, body, mind and spirit."

"Release the trauma, make decisions, be the inner child."

"So mote it be!"

Stella found herself joining in, as if she knew the words as well.

A LOUD BANG WOKE STELLA up. She jumped up and went to check on the kids.

"Damn! Of course," she frowned as she remembered they weren't there. Even after nearly five years, she sometimes forgot they weren't tucked up safely in their beds.

Still half-lost in the dream, she wandered around, trying to find the source of the noise.

The back door was wide open.

"What the? How did that happen? I know I shut and locked that door."

She grabbed her packet of cigarettes from the planter pot, turned on the kettle, and sat outside in the moonlight.

"I have no idea how that door swung open. I mustn't have shut or locked it properly after all."

"I know that was just a dream, but it felt so real. The words made sense. I loved being a mum to those beautiful kids, teaching them, playing with them, creating a life with them."

Stella looked around for the frog.

On this hot summer's evening, by the light of the full moon, so close to Christmas, she could feel a shift in the energy, like something magical was going to happen.

Stella lit a candle, took another cigarette out of the packet, promising to quit again tomorrow.

"If you are real, my spirit guides, and if you are listening to me. I know my kids are grown up, but I want them back. I want to spend time with them." Remembering the words from the dream, she added, "So mote it be."

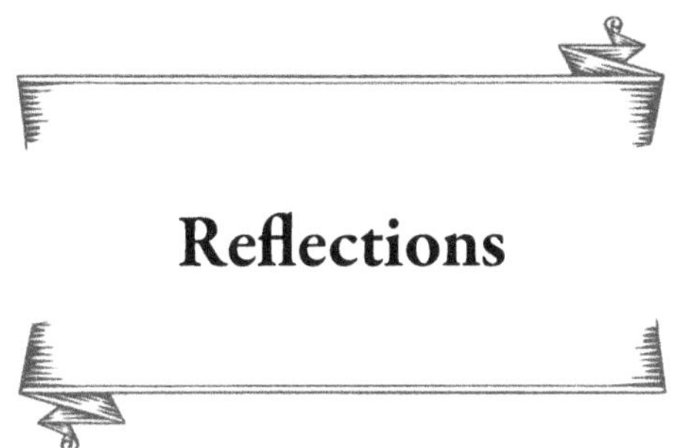

Reflections

S tella

When the children were little, Christmas time was the best. Making advent calendars, decorations for the tree and the house. Stella had knitted a nativity set, Santa and Mrs Santa and many other characters. She loved seeing the looks of love and wonder on her children's faces at Christmas time.

"I tried so hard to make Christmas full of wonder and excitement, creating Christmas memories. It seems like such a very long time ago."

After the rift, Christmas time was the worst. Christmas without her children was like part of her was missing. She was so grateful for her wonderful friends who made sure she wasn't alone over the holidays. They included her in their family Christmas traditions.

"That first Christmas, when the kids spent Christmas with their dad and his family, that was the worst! I know they had grandparents, aunts and uncles, cousins, all the family interactions I had missed out on as a child. I know I said I didn't want them to miss out on family stuff like I did, but I wish I had fought for more time with them."

Moving back into the house, she continued, noticing the envelopes sitting in a pile on the kitchen bench.

"Maybe then they would visit ME at Christmas, and I could decorate the house like we used to!" Stella threw the pile of unopened Christmas cards in frustration and watched them fall flat on the floor rather than landing with a thud anywhere.

"Next time, I will throw something heavier," she laughed to herself as she picked them up. Her obsessive-compulsive disorder hated mess, whether anyone else was around to witness it or not.

"I know I told them that anytime we spend time together is special, and it is, but still, I would love just one Christmas celebration, one year," Stella muttered, more disappointed in herself than anyone else.

A loud bang distracted her. Going to investigate, she found the portable clothes dryer had fallen over onto the vacuum cleaner. The tangled mess was taunting her.

"So what knocked that over?" Stella couldn't see any obvious culprit.

"I get it, okay?" she said to the ether. "I like everything tidy, but when I tidy the house and it stays tidy, it makes me sad. That doesn't mean it is okay to mess things up for me to tidy up."

As she stacked the vacuum back into the wardrobe, she remembered that first time when her children spent the holidays with their dad. Stella had tidied the house, and it stayed tidy. She hated it. Hated how quiet the house was without those beautiful bundles of joy.

The clothes dryer leant back against the wall. Stella took a deep breath and decided to open the Christmas cards.

"It's not their fault I hate Christmas. I am the Christmas Grinch!" Stella jumped up onto the lounge, standing on the lounge, shaking her fist in the air.

Tears welled up in her eyes as she read the Christmas greetings from her friends. Stella sighed and sat down, wiping her footprints off the purple suede lounge. The best second-hand furniture bargain ever.

STELLA USED WRITING as a form of therapy. She had to write down her feelings to release the feeling of pain and regret. Otherwise, it would eat her alive.

"I have to write something, or I will just drink the rest of that cask. And I really need to get a pet so I don't turn into the crazy old lady talking to myself."

People have commented that my world ended when my dad died, and yes, it was a defining moment. For me though, my world fell apart the day my children went with their father and his family. My children were my world, my life, and the reason why I existed. Everything I did, I did for them.

Stella paused, wondering how she ever thought she would be able to successfully parent without a family network for support.

I missed those social cues. I did try to remedy this and provide a supportive social network for my own children. I underestimated the impact of a lack of functional family.

The generational curse.
I didn't know that I was taking away their childhood innocence.
Stella looked up. She needed to go for a walk before it got dark.

"Not that I mind walking at night. The darkness hides the big hill I have to walk up to get back home. It is my favourite time of day. Peace and quiet to reflect." She knew how important it was not to get stuck living in the past, living with regret. As she walked around the block, past the local high school, a variety of houses, all built at least thirty years ago, she realised something.

"The only thing that stays the same is change." She didn't care who thought she was crazy, walking along, gesticulating animatedly. "Just in one generation, there has been so much change. Technology and gadgets," she pointed at the telephone booth ahead, "how we communicate and travel." As a jet flew past, so high up, all she could see was the white trail it left behind. "Even my laptop, my phone, which I take for granted. None of those things existed when Mum and Dad were growing up."

An old white sedan with P plates and a group of teenagers hanging out the back sped past, cutting the corner. Stella was pleased she had decided to wait to cross the road. Suddenly she wanted to get home. She hurried back without stopping anymore.

Back at home, she couldn't shake the feeling that something was wrong. Her spidery senses telling her something was going to happen. She quickly texted her youngest, Andie, as she was probably the only one who would answer.

Beep beep. Her phone went no more than five seconds after she sent the text. A quick glance reassured her that all the kids were safe and sound, enjoying all the trappings of spending the holidays with grandparents.

"The kids are all okay, thank goodness." Stella was relieved. Her intuition and sixth sense had been growing stronger recently. She would often feel emotions and feelings and even health issues like a headache or tummy ache. Knowing the feelings weren't hers and not understanding what was wrong drove her crazy.

"Being an empath has its advantages," Stella thought. "Especially now I know what that means. No wonder I don't like being around large groups of people." She eyed the cask of wine as she opened the fridge but opted instead for some green juice. A mix of apple, ginger, cucumber, kale, spinach and pear. She took her diary outside with her juice and watched the sun set behind the pine trees and hedge at the back of the rental property.

Feelings and emotions.

Everyone has experienced loss of loved ones.

Devastation, loss through fire, famine, flood, family illness or family break ups.

Arguments and trauma.

We all struggle to make sense of life and find our place in the world, in the family.

These challenges have been the same for all generations.

We heal through understanding and letting go.

We can make the change and create a happier future.

We all struggle with demons.

Parents not coping, lack of support, lack of knowledge of how to parent, cook, clean, and look after each other and ourselves.

Addictions, trauma, drama, pain.

None of us are suffering alone.

Stella stopped writing. Too much emotion. Time for healing. Choosing peppermint tea instead of a mug of cask white wine was a struggle, but she was determined to follow her intuition and get healthier.

Giving into the whisperings, instead of the cravings, was a new concept, but she was willing to listen to her spirit guides and learn and heal.

If there was a way to lift this curse, to heal the generational trauma, she was determined to find it.

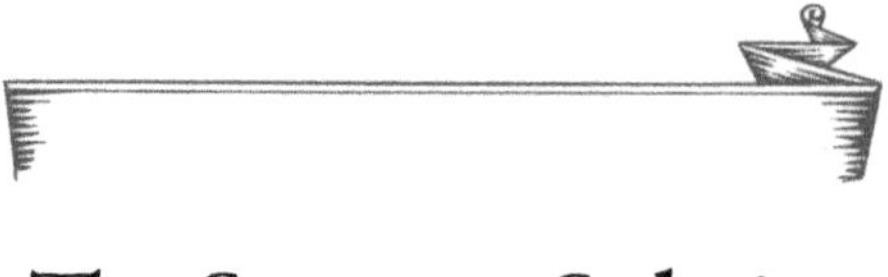

The Summer Solstice

Luna
Luna shivered. She looked up from her garden, where she had been weeding a neglected sheltered corner, hidden from sunlight by the large gum tree and the older gnarly pine cone tree. She had underplanted native bushes, tea trees and banksias, which were growing well, even without the optimum mix of sunlight and water. Clouds covered the sun, the temperature had dropped at least two degrees. She looked around for Salem and found him curled up in the pile of leaves she had raked up ages ago. The last time she had ventured this far into the darkest corner of the garden.

"It had to be done," she confided to Salem. "Ignoring the weeds won't make them go away. Let's get some more done before darkness falls."

History has a funny way of repeating itself, even when we strive to avoid the mistakes of our ancestors.

Luna stretched. And stood up suddenly. As healing as garden work was, she knew when to call it quits for the day. Her muscles ached as she scooped Salem up from his newfound cushion of leaves and meandered through the lavender, rosemary, basil and feverfew, all big bushes now; how many years old she couldn't remember. She loved brushing past them and smelling their healing gift of scent.

As it was already cool, Luna closed her door behind her. She turned on the light. Not feeling like jumping at shadows tonight, and she hated wearing her spectacles, big old wonky round glasses that made her look like a school principal. It was time for some incense and candles. Tonight the crone needed to cleanse and release, light the way for the spirits, and let go of the ghosts from so very long ago.

Celebrations and family – waves of emotions and extremes

In Australia, midsummer celebrations are extremely poignant, so close to Christmas. We are blessed with long hot days. Children are on holidays, and lucky parents and grandparents are also on holidays, to spend precious time with family.

But what about all those people who aren't so blessed?

Midsummer celebrates the season of the sun, where the plants and flowers and animals revel in the warmer days. In Australia, there are droughts, raging fires, and even floods. A time and place of extremes. A time of extreme emotions and drama, arguments and stress, anxiety, and love and laughter as well.

Feasts and celebrations with loved ones. A time of growth and abundance. A time to honour the energy of the sun, connect with the natural world and celebrate the abundance of the earth.

Stella

Stella knew it was partly her lack of confidence that sabotaged her. She yearned for that feeling of connection and community. She did have friends, but lost connection with some who felt awkward when Stella lost her children. Others stopped visiting when Stella started talking about crystals, essential oils and angel cards.

"Who am I now? I don't have my children, but I am still a mother. I am not married, I am not who I was before. I don't go to church anymore. I believe in a whole other spiritual realm now."

How could she expect to make connections with others when she didn't yet know how to connect with herself?

Luna

"It's funny that I prefer my own company now, as I am getting older." Luna lit the row of coloured candles on her altar. Pink, purple, green, yellow, orange, red and blue tea light candles she found in the local grocers. Using one match was tricky, but she was getting better at it. The crone saved her matches like she saved so many little things. She could always re-purpose and reuse them.

"One sage incense cone left," Luna said to Salem. "I must remember to grab some more next time I see incense at the shop."

She watched the flames dance and create shadows on the back wall.

"I have spent many years with others and many alone. I used to think I needed to celebrate with my coven." Patting Salem as his little paws needled her lap, she continued, "And now I choose to celebrate alone." She paused, "Probably because of the Christmas rift. The curse that broke my family so many years ago." She glanced at the photo of Freddie, Annie, Lizzie and Katie, taken so long ago. Tears welled in her eyes. She blinked them away.

STELLA

Stella closed her eyes, slowly breathing in and exhaling, counting her breaths. She had read that counting breaths, concentrating on breathing, had health benefits. At the very least, she hoped it would calm and help her sleep.

In the dark, behind her closed eyes, she saw flashes of a scene as if she was watching a movie. Three women in black robes walked through a forest, either at dusk or dawn. She couldn't tell which; all she could see was the sun low down behind the trees. The trees looked different, not eucalypts or trees she was used to seeing. The undergrowth was not typical Australian grass and weeds either. This was thicker, lower and fluffy or spongy. She was so engrossed in figuring out the flora that when one of the women raised her hands, Stella jumped and opened her eyes. She quickly closed them again, wanting to know what happened next. Nothing.

Ten minutes later, sipping her cup of green tea, she thought about what she had seen. Three women in robes who seemed somehow familiar. A forest of some kind, with flora that was foreign to her.

Was she simply remembering a television show or movie she had watched, or a book she had read? She was curious. She closed her eyes, trying to get back to that scene. In the darkness, she didn't see a thing, but she heard voices. As she listened, she pictured a coven of witches chanting as they cast spells.

She hoped it wasn't the Christmas curse.

She hoped it might be the solution to the curse that she was listening to.

A few days later, Stella sat at the kitchen bench, thinking back over that strange afternoon. Did she believe that witchcraft existed? Was it possible to cast a spell to cure the curse?

She looked at the little figurine of a little goth fairy dressed in purple and black. A gift from her dad many years ago. She had moved it into the kitchen after her weird dream. It sat next to her laptop.

"I am pretty sure I can't cast a spell and bring my children back. It is against their free will, and I don't ever want to do that," Stella told her little fairy friend.

"If I was a witch, one of my rules would be to harm no one."

Each time she looked at it, she swore the little figure had changed ever so slightly. Her hands seemed to be in different positions. Even the way she sat on her toadstool seemed to change. Stella wasn't sure what to make of that either, but she was too distracted to give the rogue fairy any serious thought.

It only takes a spark of belief to start a chain reaction for good.

By lighting this candle I call on spirits past and present
To guide my way, out of darkness and shame,
Out of regret and pain
To a world of new beginnings and love
A world where anything is possible if we believe hard enough
Setting intentions for a life of love, connections, family,
Relationships that are healthy and loving and giving.
The best way of living
As it is now and in the future, So mote it be.

Addictions, Narcissists and the Inner Child

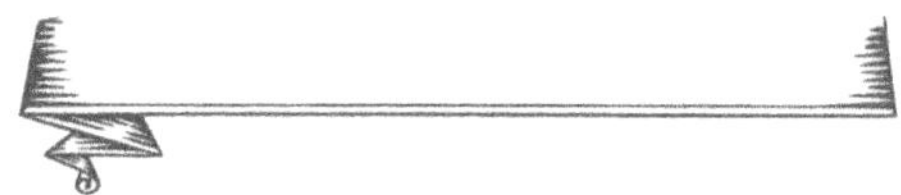

Is an addiction something that catches us when we fail to think something through, or is it when we think too much and we cloud our reason and good judgement?

Luna

These days, lighting incense, lighting candles, and gardening were Luna's only addictions. She vaguely remembered a time when she was caught up in the ways of the world, the material world. Technology, drugs, modern medicine, drama and glamour.

Lighting the sage smudge stick to cleanse the negative energy in her cottage always reminded her of detoxing and cleansing her mind, body and soul.

"I know I was easily led and got caught up with a bad crowd. I wasted so much money on poker machines, cigarettes and alcohol. It was an intoxicating mix. I am so glad I swapped all that for a much simpler life." Maude poked her head inside to see who her crone was talking to.

"It took a total breakdown in health and wellness, a hospital stay and months of recovery." She confided to Maude.

"I was still young then. I journeyed in search for knowledge of the old ways, healing and for like-minded souls. I became Crone after my adventures through the realms."

"It started when I discovered I could control my interactions with people in my dreams. The dreams got even more intense when I stopped drinking and smoking. Somehow in my dreams, I could cross over to other realms and times past, when witches roamed the earth." Maude had tiptoed inside, loving the sound of the crone's voice.

"Oh how we danced! We created magic and mayhem and manipulating energy." Luna shuffled around the cottage, bumping into her chair and her desk as she swirled and danced. "We travelled through realms. We helped and healed so many people." The crone fondly remembered her friends and fellow witches Catherine and Tizzie. There were others, but the power of three was stronger with these women.

Lammas is the witch festival of the harvest was a reminder of the old ways. Before electricity and refrigeration, people would harvest vegetables and grain and store them for the cooler months. Baking bread, cooking a feast, pickling fruits and vegetables, making sure families were fed over the winter. Back in a time when people paid attention to the earth, its cycles and patterns.

Lammas in Australia is on the first of February. It is the first of three harvest festivals. The first fruits of the summer are ripe and ready. Grain is ready for gathering.

A time to give thanks for the blessings of the earth and to honour life and death.

A time to celebrate and share the harvest with family and friends.

Luna

For a witch living alone with her animal family, Luna didn't cook much. She ate the food she grew herself. Sometimes she brought yoghurt, chocolate or savoury snacks.

"I do prefer to limit processed foods though."

Luna was in her garden, collecting the herbs she loved so much.

"I love eating these, drying them, making teas and other potions and lotions." This time it was an orb spider Luna had stepped to avoid who was listening to her. She had spent the morning collecting her favourites. Her baskets were full.

"Peppermint, lavender, sage, rosemary, oregano, thyme, calendula, echinacea, feverfew, basil, comfrey, borage and yarrow."

The brown twine was so old and frayed parts of it almost disintegrated as she hung herb bundles from the rafters on her side verandah, the side sheltered from most of the weather. Smiling at the fragrances wafting around her. Luna was content with the life she was creating for herself now. She was surprised when she heard herself humming. Celebrations of harvest, of survival, of healing those addictions. It all seemed like such a long time ago. These days her inhibitions and inner child seemed to pop in and out unannounced even more often. The crone wondered if she was going crazy or at the start of the dementia path.

"You are celebrating the child in you, your inner child. You aren't crazy or demented. It is difficult for you, as you never had the opportunity as a child, to be a child."

Luna nodded. Her guides were right there. Growing up all those years ago, there had been no opportunity to play or laugh. Survival had been the key.

"But it wasn't all bad," she whispered back.

"We know. We were there then as we are here now. We will always look out for you." Luna didn't bother looking for the body responsible for the voice. She knew her guides rarely manifested as humans anymore. They didn't need to. She was quite happy to talk to them, her spirit friends, as she had talked to her imaginary friends all those years ago.

STELLA

"I know my addictions are my way of coping with stress." She looked at the packet of cigarettes and the coffee mug full of wine on the glass table in front of her.

"I know it is because I don't think I can cope that I drink and smoke. I also know that I probably do this because it is what I watched Mum and Dad do.

"I didn't consciously make the decision to mimic the behaviour I witnessed growing up."

She held a cigarette in her right hand, trying to decide whether to light it or not.

"I really want to, but I know that it is because it is an addiction, not a need.

"What if I just threw all my cigarettes and wine away?" Stella asked the big pot of basil and tomatoes she had growing near her outdoor setting.

"Smoking and drinking became a habit for Mum and Dad. Like eating or sleeping. I don't want to be like that." It was normal to see her mum and dad smoke at least fifteen to twenty cigarettes each day, sitting at the dining table or in the chairs in the lounge room. Each marble table beside its plush black leather armchair held its own ashtray. Two of the tables also held little boxes that stored cigarettes. Each day, in the late afternoon before dinner, her mum would have a sherry, and dad would have a whisky. During dinner they would have wine. Every night.

Stella placed the cigarette back into its packet. She placed the packet under her chair. She picked up her coffee mug and tipped it out into the closest plant pot. The little black one with the spider plant in it. She picked up her journal and purple pen.

> *I know I started drinking and smoking when things were stressful, during the rift.*

> *I thought that I was handling things totally differently than my parents.*

> *Every day I walked. I ate plenty of fruits and vegetables.*

> *I thought I was modelling positive behaviours to my children.*

> *I would have been better off modelling an emotional breakdown rather than desperately trying to hide it.*

In the beginning, Stella only smoked and drank when the kids were with their father or already in bed asleep. Hiding the addictive behaviour.

> *As the addictions both took hold, I could no longer hide my drinking and smoking from my children. But still, I thought I was holding it all together.*

Stella paused, looking back over what she had written.

It was five years since the rift.

"It must be time to stop feeling sorry for myself." Stella stood up, pushing the metal chair back. She picked up the metal watering can from under the table.

"Here you go, little spider plant," she said, giving the plant a big drink of water. She felt bad she had poured her wine into the pot.

Now that she was taking positive steps to confront and heal her addictive behaviours, it felt like she was opening the curtains and seeing the world outside, clearly, for the first time in a long time.

She noticed the rose bush that she had planted in the blue ceramic pot was flowering.

"Hello, you beautiful little lady. You are such a beautiful red. I am so glad you are flowering. When I can, I will plant some more and have a whole rose garden planted in honour of my children."

"If I had spent my money back then, when they left, on plants instead of on cigarettes and wine, I would have a whole farm full of flowering plants!"

"I was grieving too much to see clearly." She watered each of her plants, all growing in pots so she could easily transplant them into the garden one day.

"I couldn't see my options. I had no confidence. So I drank and smoked. I gave in to the big bullies, the scary yelling people. I retreated in my pain." Tears welled in her eyes as Stella moved towards the last plant, the Japanese maple. Pedro's tree. She was so pleased that the big tree they had planted when their first child was born had given her a tiny baby tree in amongst her strawberries. She had lovingly and carefully transplanted it and kept it alive for the last five years.

"I know I pretended I was holding it all together. While I was inwardly falling apart."

A rustling noise distracted Stella. It sounded like something was moving in the hedge. Curious, she turned off the tap and went to check. The hedge looked the same as always. Prickly, unfriendly, bearing little red berries and white flowers. The hedge was a mix of a few plants that Stella didn't know the names of. Not native trees, but those commonly found in most backyards. The berry tree the birds loved. The small white flowering hedge that smelled horrible. A couple of tall thin pencil pines as well. She did love the big pine cone tree in the corner. It had provided many pine cones over the years. Decorated with tinsel and adorned the Christmas time, before the rift.

"No more of the past," Stella admonished herself. "Now, what's going on with this hedge?"

Apart from the rustling noises, which she put down to birds or maybe mice hidden in the depths of the overgrown back hedge, nothing seemed out of place.

"Should I prune this?" remembering she had gotten into trouble for pruning another bush that never grew back, she decided to leave it to the landlord to sort out.

Stella looked at her cigarettes on the way back in to make a cuppa. She didn't feel like one at the moment. Maybe she was beating her addictions after all!

"Everything in moderation, my fairy friend. If I have coffee now, I will have water or green tea later. See, it's not just about wine and smokes, drugs or gambling. Sugary foods and drinks, computer games, even shopping, exercise and sport are addictive."

Stella stared at the fairy, daring it to move. She laughed at herself when she finally took her eyes away to make her coffee. When she glanced back, she was sure her fairy friend had moved, leaning forward more than before as if listening to Stella.

Stella shrugged and continued, finding it useful to speak aloud about this.

"Take exercise as an example. People take up exercise to get fit or to stay fit. Sometimes they want to excel in a sport. That sounds perfectly reasonable, doesn't it? There are other people who use exercise or sports to push or punish themselves. For whatever reason, pain, trauma, or they doubt themselves, or are victims of bullying or narcissism."

This time when she glanced back at her little friend, she appeared to be facing Stella but in the yoga pose.

"Hmm...I am going to ignore that. I am not going crazy."

"Now where was I up to? Oh yes, that's right."

"I think it is about finding that healthy balance. Our state of mind, our mental health plays such a big role in why we do what we do.

"Some of us never get past what happened when we were young. Others seem to be able to shrug off the insults and live fairly well-adjusted, happy lives."

Dreams and Memories

Luna

The crone was feeling light-headed. She realised she hadn't slept much the night before. She had been caught up in a dream where portals were opening and closing. People were moving about, and she woke up with a sense of dread mixed with anticipation.

"The last time I remember feeling like this, I was with Catherine and Tizzie," Luna mused as she made her morning cup of coffee. Salem jumped up on the table, looking for some milk.

"Hop down, you know better than that." She gently lifted him down, filling his saucer with the milk she was going to pour into her cup. The cat eagerly lapped up the milk, which he received as a treat, maybe once a week or so, depending on how much Luna had left the day before her trek to the shop in the village. It was a few days before the next shopping expedition, but Luna was distracted.

To make matters worse, there seemed to be more shadows than normal floating around just out of reach of her vision. Even Salem seemed more jumpy, and he was the most chilled of all the crone's familiars.

Although it was still warm and early in the morning, Luna lit a fire to talk to her friends. These days it was one of the easiest ways, especially if her dreams were becoming muddled.

"Dear friend! We were going to come and find you today," Catherine and Tizzie appeared as soon as she got the fire started. She didn't even have to add any sticks. They arrived as soon as the flames danced in the newspaper.

"We tried to reach you in your dreams, but there was a fog. We think the portals are opening again. The problem is, we don't know where."

"Why do you think they are opening?" Luna was surprised, worried, and also a little excited by the concept of being able to easily travel between worlds again.

"The animals are restless. The fairies, elves and sprites are on the move. We are hearing stories of a new and powerful witch. Someone who is only just now beginning to learn about her powers," Tizzie responded.

"What do you need me to do?"

"Nothing for now," replied Catherine. "We will keep you up to date. Just be careful and be on the lookout for strange occurrences."

"I will do! You both stay safe too," she whispered as her sisters were already leaving the embers that were left of the fire.

"Fiddlesticks. I forgot to add the twigs." Eyeing the pile of sticks and twigs, she decided not to call them back. "You never know when I might need to call them again," she told Salem, who was sitting attentively next to her.

"I must remember to get my spell book out and practice," Luna said. "After I plant some more seeds," Luna loved the cooler weather autumn brought. It was the perfect weather to plant seeds in the potting mix in the greenhouse she had made from leftover pipes, star pickets and shade cloth. After having to rebuild it several times, Luna had rebuilt the structure in a more sheltered area between two big eucalypts. Today she was planting fennel, coriander, parsley and basil.

"With any luck, I will be eating them all by mid-winter." Luna was quite content, with her only vices being her garden, plants and fresh herbs and spices. She felt giggly like a child as she skipped along her path to the greenhouse. Dementia or second childhood. She was never really sure.

Stella

The sudden gust of wind made Stella clench her hands into tight fists. She didn't like the wind. Windy days made her cranky. Windy days and stormy days drove her children, and the children where she worked, crazy too.

"I don't think I am normally this bad-tempered," she mused, although she did like the line from a movie she watched years ago about having been in a bad mood for the last forty years. At thirty-five she had first tried to give up cigarettes—for health reasons—but also to set a better example for her children. Each time she tried, she found herself getting more and more bad-tempered and so she started smoking again.

"I tell myself it is so I am less cranky with my kids, but I don't know that it's quite true. Especially now they don't even live with me anymore.

"I must be crazy. It is so windy today! Standing out here, in the freezing wind, trying to light my cigarette is nearly impossible!" she moaned to her rose geranium, newly re-potted into a fancy blue ceramic pot.

At nearly forty, none of her children lived with her full-time. Pedro and Kay, both adults now, didn't spend any time with her. Emily and Andie both visited occasionally, in between school, sport and friends. They mostly lived with their dad. Stella cherished what time she did get to spend with her children.

Aware of the fact that Emily and Andie might be coming for a visit in about an hour, and as far as she knew, they still didn't know she was smoking again, she quickly sucked on her smoke once it was lit. Finishing it in record time, she tucked the stub away in the bottom of the stack of empty pots.

Once inside, her cigarettes and lighter were hidden in the makeup bag at the bottom of her underwear drawer. Stella changed her clothes, sprayed deodorant, cleaned her teeth and chewed on some mints, ready to welcome her kids home.

Luna

Luna had grown to love windy days like this. It had taken her nearly her whole sixty-five years to do so.

"I was such a nerd, so long ago, I had to have the answer to everything," she told Maude as she fed her. "Science says windy days stir up the ions in the air. Sensitive souls, empaths and children, for example, feel agitated by this change. I used to hate the February and August winds. The winds of change." She smiled, remembering how she used to scurry back inside, moaning that she couldn't be outside, working in her garden on windy days. In some places she had lived, that meant whole weeks inside, every time she ventured out, gusts of wind buffeted her.

"I never enjoyed being stuck inside, so I eventually decided wind wasn't so bad after all."

She glanced across at her *Book of Spells* sitting where she had left it, where she had been reading in the morning sunshine.

"When I discovered that witches generally loved windy days as the wind washed away negativity, cleansing the air, cleansing us too, I was blown away."

Maude patiently listened, waiting for the last of the seed the crone was holding in her hand. "I learnt how to harness the power of the wind in spell work. Being outside, letting the wind blow away everything I was holding on to that I didn't need.

"Although, if I am honest," Luna mused, "I still don't like windy days. My bad moods are always worse in the wind. Or is it a habit I can't control, or don't want to control?"

Maude finished her seed and flew off to find some bugs. Luna was lost in her thoughts and didn't notice that she was by herself.

"I am no longer interested in soul searching or working on my inner child, or my moods. I don't have to get along with anyone."

Many years ago, she was a totally different person. As maiden and mother, it was easy to be there for her children. She loved being a mother, teaching them the ways of the world. Then the rift broke her whole universe, taking her children away forever. One day they were there, and the next, gone. Devastated that she hadn't been able to keep her children safe, she made bad choice after bad choice, fuelled by anxiety and depression, devastation at the loss of her family, the only family she had ever known.

Loud banging interrupted Luna's walk down memory lane. She looked around for the source of the banging. "Over here," offered a muffled voice.

As Luna opened the lid of Maude's birdseed bin, the angriest elf she had seen for a long time jumped out, coughing as birdseed flew everywhere.

"How on earth?"

"Don't you how on earth me!" the elf retorted. "You were so busy lost in your self-pity you didn't even see me." The elf continued as he jumped up onto the rocking chair arm, holding his balance as it rocked back and forth.

"If I hadn't interrupted you, you would be remembering all the bullies and abuse you suffered. All those nasty men who treated you like rubbish. They treated all women like rubbish. Even the witches. It wasn't just you, sister!" The elf was so gruff, and the crone was so put out by his behaviour, he continued uninterrupted.

"They were narcissists and bullies. They knew better. You didn't. What you don't know is they all met a grizzly end. Eventually. That's what elves are for."

Luna finally found her voice, "So why did I have to lose my soul mate too? He was so gentle and kind. Considerate but also intelligent and magic and mystical. He wasn't afraid or angry or tough." She had yelled at the moon for months to help her find people who were like her. She had called on goddesses to bring her soul mates. She had focused on a version of her life where she was safe and loved and happy. Little did she know she was creating a powerful spell.

The elf looked at her. "You know why. Magic comes at a cost. Your wizard prince did find you. You had ten beautiful, happy and carefree years with him."

Her eyes welled with tears. "Yes, we were in love. We were blessed and married, and it was the best time ever. But too short." She had tried to be the best person she could be for him. Her prince asked for nothing in return for loving her.

"Why only ten years?"

"Think of it the other way. You had ten marvellous years. Most people never get that. The same with your children. You are their mother, always. You did spend time with them. Things happen for a reason. The reasons may never be known.

"That's not why I am here," the elf slid down to the seat of the chair, causing it to rock even more. Salem, who had been watching warily from behind Luna's boots, was ready to pounce to protect his crone if needed.

"Salem, stop. He is our friend, I think."

"My name is Edward, I know, Eddie the Elf," he rolled his eyes. "I bring a message from the realms."

Luna crouched down to make eye contact with Eddie, "Nice to meet you, Eddie."

"Yeah, yeah, okay. So do you want the message or not?"

"Okay, yes I do, please."

"Magic is coming back. Be prepared," he said with a flourish of his arm.

"Is that it?"

"What more do you want!" he retorted. "Magic is coming. Be prepared. The end." He jumped off the chair and started walking towards the trees at the back of her house. He paused and turned back, "One more thing. Get all your tears and regrets out of the way. You will need to focus." With that, as quickly as he arrived, Eddie the elf vanished.

"Did I dream that?" she asked Salem as she scooped him up in one hand and her book and cup in the other. Salem shook his head no.

"Then I had better get to work." She let her eyes wander to the ancestor wall.

"Remember."

"Believe."
"Trust."

The whispers, the voices from the ancestor wall, her beautiful wizard prince and the others. They all supported her, whispering encouragement from their side of the realms. Years ago, she had begun hearing voices and seeing beings from beyond the grave. Now, more than twenty years sober, she knew they were as real as she was. As real as Eddie the Elf.

"I do love being alone. Only because I don't have to be on my best behaviour," she told her wizard. "I can be cranky, or crazy, without being scared of getting it wrong. I know you always loved me being a free spirit. You taught me so much. I can't wait to see you again." She blew kisses at the photo on the wall. "I know I have to wait. That's okay. It will make our reunion so much more awesome."

Most of her loved ones on the wall spoke to her at least several times a year. She was used to hearing them now and wasn't scared.

The only thing was, she had never heard the voices of her children. She guessed they were in another realm and all grown with lives of their own. Would she change anything if it meant she could see her children again? If she could be part of their lives? She struggled with this thought. Every time she tried to focus on bringing back Freddie, Annie, Lizzie and Katie, she was clearly told...

"No."

Although she begged and pleaded and implored, "No" was all she ever got.

She could still see them, as clearly as if they were standing in front of her right now. She still talked to them every day. She didn't know if they could hear her. She did know that she had given birth to them for a reason, and if the reason was for them to be born and then to move somewhere else, at least she had been able to look after them for a short time. That was a blessing.

She lit a candle at her altar. Straightening the photos, shuffling them around so that her kids' faces were at the front with her wizard prince. She crushed some rosemary in her mini cast iron cauldron, added some sage and lit it as she chanted.

Ancestors, family, soul mates past, present and future...
Help me to live and grow, learn and love...
Harm no one, help all...
So mote it be...

MAUDE SCREECHED OUTSIDE, waking Luna from where she was lost in memories.

"Hang on, Maude. I know I have already fed you. Before our visitor. I can't come out in the garden today. I have to prepare for magic, before I forget."

Her *Book of Spells* was still a work in progress. It probably always would be. She doubted there would be a point in time when she would be satisfied with her life's work. Annotating her journey through the craft of being a witch. Her knowledge of spells and witchery was forever growing. She grew more aware of the world of magic. Her awakening began many years before she found herself in her cottage. There was no doubt though, that her magic grew stronger here each day.

The crone looked up. She was so proud of her little cottage and her garden. A rickety old shed, many years ago, her cottage was a little bigger than a double garage is today. Old timber floors, worn with dust and dirt, lined with modern-day gyprock for walls and a ceiling. Wind chimes made from old kitchen cutlery, an old wooden broomstick, some pans and three dream catchers hung from the wooden beam attached along the middle of the ceiling of the main room. The main living area was an eclectic mix of kitchen, altar room, sitting room and dining room. A simple kitchen sink and workbench, fridge and pantry along one wall, a window peeping out over the garden. Every day, Luna watched the birds in the conifers as she washed up her single plate, cup, bowl, knife and fork. The rest of the room contained a single lounge chair, an old school teacher's desk and chair, a small round dining table, a wall full of books and an altar wall.

The second room was split into a room with a shower and toilet and her bedroom. Simple, uncomplicated, just the way she liked it.

Dreams and Portals

S tella

Stella woke up as her alarm beeped that it was time to get up and ready for work. She loved her job as room leader at the preschool, but this morning, she had been deeply enveloped in a dream where she was in the forest, watching the three women.

This time Stella could tell that it was nighttime. She could see the full moon behind the trees. She watched as the women lit a small fire and raised their hands to the moon. She listened as they chanted in a language she didn't recognise. She had a feeling that she belonged in the scene, but she didn't try to move into the clearing and join the women. Just as she was deciding whether or not to approach the group, the alarm jolted her back.

Working with a room full of three and four-year-olds, Stella didn't get to think about her dream again until later that evening. Straight after finishing work, Stella had spent precious time with her youngest child, driving her to and from basketball practice.

"Why do you have that sitting there?" Andie asked, pointing at the goth fairy when they called in to grab a snack on the way to practice.

"I have to have someone here to talk to when you are with your dad," she smiled, hugging Andie.

"Aww Mum. Maybe we need to get you a cat, or a bird."

"Sounds perfect, just not fish. Fish are icky,"

Stella loved the banter between them and cherished the time they spent together.

MUCH LATER, WHEN SHE was sitting at her laptop, she remembered the dream, which seemed like so long ago.

"It was just a dream. I mean, what else could it have been?" she didn't expect the fairy to answer her, but Stella again looked at it, wondering if it actually did move.

"Nah, that is even more ridiculous than my dream not really being a dream." This time when she glanced back at the figure, it had turned away from her. Stella didn't think her statue had turned its back because she didn't believe it was real. Besides, she was still thinking about the dream. Those women looked so familiar. And she felt drawn to them somehow. She felt like she would have walked up to them if the dream had lasted a few minutes longer.

"So how do I get back to that same place as I left in my dream?" she wondered.

"Maybe I just try and remember everything that led up to that place in the dream, and I will be able to finish the dream."

As Stella got up to go to bed, she didn't notice that the statue was turned back, facing her, watching her as she left the room.

Stella closed her eyes. She focused on remembering every detail of the dream the night before. The forest, the trees, the moon behind the trees. The three women, whom she was going to call witches because she didn't know what else to call them, were there chanting and walking around the fire, their hands held high. Stella peeped around from one of the trees where she watched.

"You can join us!" called out one of the women without turning around. Stella froze, not sure what to do next.

"I don't remember your name, but I know we have met before. Maybe in another lifetime we were in a coven together."

STELLA STOOD STILL. She wasn't scared. She was listening, trying to decide her next move.

"We aren't going to hurt you. We would like you to join us in celebrating the harvest, the Lammas. Toasting the bread we have made in our fire."

Slowly Stella walked over to where the women were standing. As she got closer, she saw they had a cauldron over the fire, with three lumps of dough fashioned into the shape of loaves. The loaves were already browning around the edges. The aroma of bread baking wafted through the forest.

"Do you make your own bread? Or grow your own grain?" Stella shook her head, not quite yet finding her voice.

"We have to. I suppose you don't need to, where you live now. If you do make your own bread, it will smell and taste amazing." The taller of the three women was speaking. She wore her long jet-black hair braided and wrapped tightly up in a bun on the top of her head.

Stella nodded. "I have always wanted to have a go at making bread. And growing all sorts of plants, medicinal herbs, things like that. I also would love to make healing potions and lotions."

"You can do all those things, in your time, as you have before," this time, the smallest women, with the fairest hair Stella had ever seen, spoke. "This might not make sense now, but it will one day, when you remember."

The other woman, with vibrant red hair, linked her arm through Stella's as she joined the women dancing and chanting around the fire.

WHEN SHE WOKE THE NEXT morning, Stella stretched, smiling as she remembered her dream. She did want to learn how to make bread and grow healing plants. She loved the reminder, in her dream, of who she was. She was sure if she had lived through various lifetimes, that intrinsic part of who she was would never change.

A spell for self-love—lighting a pink or white candle.

> *Start with a pinch of pink salt.*
> *Add three rose quartz chips.*
> *A fistful each of rose petals and lavender—Into a jar,*
> *Add our intentions for self-love, self-confidence, forgiving ourselves...*
> *Believe in myself—so mote it be.*

Look for the Signs

There are messages hidden in plain sight. Everywhere. Do we notice the subtle and not-so-subtle messages the universe tries so desperately to guide us to? Or do we wonder around in not so blissful ignorance of the good, bad and ugly that surrounds us?

Luna

Magic and witchcraft. Steeped in mystery and laden with signs and symbols called sigils. Like a secret code for magic folk. As a child, Luna loved puzzles. She spent days poring over codes and games, and she always solved the hidden codes and puzzles.

As crone, she loved creating sigils and hidden meanings on hand made tarot cards and runes. The tarot cards she created from paper, she recycled and made herself. The runes she made from wood from branches that fell from trees on her property. She hand-carved the round runes and burnt the symbols on with a wood-burning tool she had discovered at a local garage sale.

Someone once suggested she could make decks of cards and sets of rune stones for profit. She had been appalled at the suggestion. Making these tools for herself was one thing; mass producing them for others just wasn't something she was interested in doing.

The sound of a cage door rattling shut made the crone jump. She swung around, wondering what she had caught in the rusty old cage now.

"Salem! Stay away from the cage. It is not meant for you."

To Luna, all animals were sacred, but foxes that tried to eat her chickens had to be relocated. The cage was a little old, rusty and rickety, and she suspected the fox could see the cage, even though she had hidden it as best she could. She, in turn, saw signs of the fox near the chicken cage, trampled undergrowth and a heap of feathers lying around. Part skill, part instinct, the dance between witch and fox.

Stella

Stella also loved those code mysteries as a child. Spending hours solving the clues and creating her own puzzles, She had spent many hours writing stories of witches and elves and fairies, all the creatures she met in the back of her mother's garden, out of sight from anyone who may have looked over the fence.

"I don't know if anyone else ever met my enchanted friends, or even if they were real. I could have imagined them, after Dad died," Stella stared at her little goth fairy, daring it to move again.

"Maybe I was still grieving dad when I got married. That might explain why I didn't realise anything was wrong until it was too late." The fairy stubbornly decided not to move. Stella's gaze moved back to her laptop.

As part of her healing, Stella had written a book, *Look for the Signs,* in the hope that her children would one day read it and understand the issues that led to their parents' separation and divorce. She hoped it might help others who were experiencing similar issues. She wrote about the signs to look for when a relationship is toxic. How to notice the clues that the relationship is unhealthy and likely to end no matter how much time and effort we put into trying to save it. She had written from a positive perspective, providing details of each of her beautiful children, their positive traits, their resilience and how much she loved them.

The feedback when she sent it for appraisal was not so positive. The recommendation was to not pursue publication of her story.

"Back then, I didn't even think about self-publishing it, or even printing a copy to keep for my children. I was just too devastated that I couldn't publish it." Stella was lost in her memories and didn't notice the fairy leaning in to listen.

"I was probably having a breakdown. I wasn't thinking clearly. I wish I had kept a copy for the kids, printed it out at least." All her pain poured out into the book that she couldn't publish.

No matter how hard she stared at it, her manuscript was not going to suddenly appear on her laptop. She had moved so many times over the last five years that if she had copied her story onto a disc or drive, she had since lost it.

"I know it is pointless to dwell on the past; the only way is forward. To forgiveness and peace." If her children ever asked her what had been in that book, she would tell them:

- For any event, there are three points of view, yours, mine and the unbiased truth of it.
- We all have different versions and memories of life events. Especially traumatic, dramatic life-changing occasions, but also mundane everyday family or work events.
- Our memories are linked to our state of mind. What other things are going on in our lives? Did we argue with someone? Are we having a bad hair day? Did we receive bad news or win the lottery? Did someone upset us, or are we in love?
- A common mechanism to cope with trauma is to block all memories, the good and the bad.
- Addictions to alcohol, cigarettes, exercise, gaming or shopping are all ways we cope with what is happening around us.
- As well as speaking my truth, I would like to hear yours.
- Our memories can be biased by another person's point of view.
- Stress and anxiety can cause a range of illnesses.
- Being an adult, balancing work, a mortgage, a family and everything else can be tricky.
- Sometimes we just can't help others, no matter how much we want to.
- It is never okay to suffer verbal abuse.

Stella jotted down some more thoughts for her journal.

Making the decision to leave and take the kids was not a decision I made lightly.

The health and wellbeing of my kids were the driving force. I was sure this was the only way to give them the best chance at a happy, balanced, carefree, safe and secure life.

Because I lost my dad at such a young age, it took me a long time to work out what to do.

Home wasn't very nice. Cranky and tired, arguing all the time. It turns out their dad was a much nicer father, and they had a much better relationship with him when I left.

In the back of the book she had chosen for her journal, Stella had placed some photos of her children when they were little. She spoke softly to their pictures as she looked at their pictures.

"I should have worked harder to keep us all together."

"In hindsight, I do wish I had made a slightly different decision. I thought I could take you all with me, but I couldn't. I wasn't there to protect you from the trauma and drama, the lies and miscommunication."

Smiling at photos of Pedro, Kay, Emily and Andie, she whispered, "I guess everything happens for a reason, and just like losing dad, maybe what happened is part of a larger plan. A plan I don't yet know or understand. I will always cherish the memories I have of each of you."

Photos of making spaghetti bolognese with Pedro. Having so much fun cutting the carrots and tomatoes, and mixing the sauce. The girls smiling as they licked the bowl after making cupcakes filled with smarties. "There were some good times when you were little, before the rift. Trips to the coast, the park, the war memorial, the beach, we had so much fun," she whispered.

A weird noise interrupted Stella's thoughts. Her laptop screen went blank. The clock on the microwave went blank as well. The power was out, again. Checking the fuse box, she flipped the fuses back on. The familiar whirr of the fridge told her the power was working again. This was the third time in as many weeks that the electricity shorted out. There was no reasonable explanation.

"There is one unreasonable explanation," she thought to herself. "Although, it is too crazy to be true. Since I have cut down on the alcohol, whenever I get emotional about the kids, or what happened to cause the rift, anything else that causes me to get upset, the power goes out." Stella was pacing, talking to herself.

She closed her laptop and reset the microwave clock, totally oblivious to the goth fairy who was following her every move. "Maybe now that I have stopped drinking alcohol and I am facing my demons and my emotions... Could I really be setting off the power? My energy aligned with the electromagnetic field or something?"

Instead of pouring herself a drink of wine, she turned on the kettle and dropped a huge teaspoon of coffee into her favourite mug, the one with the ginger kitten. There was no point dwelling on the past. Stella couldn't change anything.

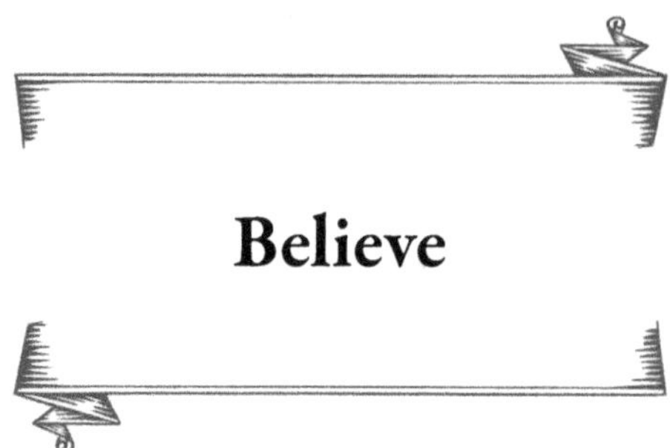

Believe

Luna

Luna jumped up with a start. She had been having that nightmare again. The one where she was caught in a giant cage, perched high up on a cliff, overlooking the countryside below. The little hamlet in the middle of the bush was being ravaged by a cranky dragon. A dirty green one with spikes all the way down its back. Big talons, like a giant eagle on all four legs. Breathing fire out of his point mouth, he was indiscriminately scaring and hurting the people below.

The crone was powerless to help.

She could see the key for her cage around the neck of the dragon. The fire the dragon was breathing had started a bush fire in what looked like a eucalypt bush scape. She always paid attention to these details in her dreams. This information tended to come in handy later on.

She frantically tried to remember the spell for rain.

Was it...

"Rain, rain, come to me, drench the land, make an inland sea."

or maybe, *"Soothing rains, please bless the earth..."*

Every time she got this far, she would wake up without resolving the dream.

She was determined to break the drought and save the people. Determined that there will be a resolution and a better life for all, whether in her dream life or in the here and now.

Belief can do so many wonderful things. It can bring people together. It can mean the difference between success and failure, health and illness, happiness and sadness.

Like the pagan celebration of Mabon, following on from Lammas, it is the thanksgiving of all the fruits of the earth. A timely reminder for this witch to let go of what she couldn't change. It is time to celebrate all the good in the world.

Stella

Stella knew her childhood had not been perfect, but that she had been fortunate in some ways. Her dad was the local dentist in a small town. Her parents were older than her parents' friends and were well off by all accounts. They lived in the mansion on the top of the hill.

When her dad passed, her mum didn't cope very well. This was when Broomhilda the Witch, Tip Top the Elf, and other fairy friends came to visit. They knew Stella needed them. She thought back over her childhood, wondering where her magical friends were now.

Stella cherished the memories of her childhood, trips to the park with her dad. Feeding the pigeons. She remembered her parents' dinner parties. She wished she could have shown her children where she had grown up. The big house with a playroom, a billiard room and a ball room with beautiful red shag plush carpet that rolled up to reveal a dance floor. She wished they could have played in the pool, and the sandpit, as she had.

Stella jumped up from her position on the purple couch.

"Enough of this!" she admonished herself.

Stella made herself a coffee and opened her laptop. While she had been investigating tools for writing and sharing files, she had stumbled across Google Docs. She used it for work all the time now. Google Docs had other benefits too. Stella could help her youngest daughter with her homework, write her own story and work on the programs for the children at the centre. She loved her laptop and how easy it was to communicate with others. She could literally pick up her laptop and take it anywhere.

Luna

Luna was only just getting used to using a computer. She wasn't even sure it was better than her old-fashioned typewriter. All her writing was done either with pen and paper, or the old typewriter she had kept for many years. She didn't even own a television anymore. Her energy seemed to play havoc with the electromagnetic fields. She didn't miss having a television. The voices and whisperings of her spirit guides were more than enough entertainment.

Stella

Stella was still having the same issues with technology. Why the television only worked when her children visited, she had no idea. She was still sure the electrical issues had something to do with her moods and emotions. She didn't miss the television. While it wasn't working, it gave her more time to investigate her new found interest in cooking and growing plants.

"My little friend, it is time for you to look after my seeds," Stella gently lifted her little goth fairy, placing her carefully in the mini hothouse she had found at the local op shop. She had filled the greenhouse with some seed-raising mix, sprinkled parsley and chive seeds in one section and peppermint and lavender in the other. If she was honest, she felt a little uneasy around the figurine. As silly as it sounded, she was certain that the figurine was always moving. Facing to the left or to the right, the fairy's pose changing ever so subtly. It made her uneasy. She gently placed the greenhouse, complete with fairy guardian, on the kitchen window sill. She was sure she saw the fairy stand up, looking around at her new surroundings.

Now her benchtop looked empty, with no little creature there to talk to. She made a mental note to look for something to put on the bench, to brighten it up, next time she was at the op shop.

She took a purple velvet pouch out of her bag. Taking out a clear quartz point, she sat it on the bench. Lighting a tea light candle, Stella concentrated on her breathing. Focused on the candle and the crystal. Trying to block out all the chatter and clutter in her brain.

As she stared at the crystal, she heard mutterings and mumbling behind her. She swung around, but of course, there was no one there. Her concentration was broken, and she suddenly felt very tired.

As she hopped into bed, snuggling under the covers, the mutterings and mumblings continued. Stella felt comforted instead of scared. As she closed her eyes, she again found herself in the forest with the three women.

THEY WERE IN A WORKSHOP. A large wooden bench filled nearly the whole room, with floor-to-ceiling shelves containing jars of what looked like herbs and seeds and bark. Her three dream friends were each at the wooden bench, cutting plants, grinding them in a mortar and pestle. Even in her dream, Stella still heard someone muttering behind her. She concentrated on watching her friends.

"Those voices are real," said the woman who spoke first last time without turning around. "They won't harm you. Your guides are just getting to know you. Soon you will hear and understand what they are saying. It will feel like a voice in your head, ideas and plans just pop in, and it will make perfect sense."

"Are these guides, ever dangerous?" Stella asked.

"No. Well, not likely. In rare cases, there are lower entities, tricksters who are malevolent. You seem to have an aura around you which keeps those types of creatures away. Your guides will only advise you for your highest good."

Stella wasn't sure how to answer. She knew it was only a dream, but it was feeling very real. She sat down on a wooden stool in the corner of the workshop. She noticed some branches shaped into walking sticks or maybe wands hanging from the ceiling beams. Half a dozen brooms of gnarled tree branches and straw lying against the far wall. Walking over, she saw the intricate details carved into the brooms. Runes, she thought, though she had no idea where that knowledge came from.

"Come and join us. We are making spell jars for Friday's market." The blonde witch beckoned.

"I don't know how, but I would love to learn." She watched for a while. "How do you know which herbs work in which jars?"

"Centuries of knowledge passed down through our covens."

"Do you write anything down, for others to learn?"

"We do, but we only share with a few people. Women like us can be misunderstood." The witch with the plaits led Stella over to a wooden chest tucked into a corner, almost hidden by the shadows.

The witch with the plaits placed the chest on a shelf, which seemed to be made solely for holding the chest. Opening the golden clasps, she lifted out a smallish leather book. Stella could tell it was well used, worn, yet she could feel the energy emanating from the book.

"We have written many things down, in many different books. We call them different things, *Grimoires, Book of Spells*, diaries or even recipe books. Each book has a purpose." The woman handed the book to Stella.

Reverently, she took the volume and opened it. Slowly turning the pages, she read the dainty print, listing ingredients for spell jars. There were jars for prosperity, happiness, insight, banishing, love, healing, success and protection.

Some of the ingredients she recognised: cinnamon, clove, lemon balm, lavender and peppermint. Others she hadn't heard of before.

GETTING READY FOR WORK the next morning, Stella was trying to remember the ingredients in the prosperity spell. She remembered cinnamon and clove, but after that, it was a little fuzzy.

"I know it's only a dream, she told her reflection in the mirror, but it would have been handy if I had been able to take a photo of some of the ingredients in that book."

A couple of minutes later, as she hopped out of the shower, she noticed the mirror had fogged up from the steam of the hot shower.

"I forgot to turn on the exhaust..." Stella stopped mid-sentence, reading the words that had appeared in the mirror: *cinnamon, clove, peppermint, chamomile, citrine, green aventurine, coins.*

"How?"

"Why?"

"Whoa! Camera." Stella grabbed her phone and took a photo of the words in the mirror before they disappeared.

At least ten times during the day, when she really shouldn't be looking at her phone during work at all, she checked to see if the photo was there or if she imagined it. The photo was there, each time.

Did this mean that her dream wasn't a dream, and if it wasn't a dream, then what was it?

Using the photo, she was able to grab all the herbs she needed for the spell jar on the way home from work. Luckily citrine and green aventurine were two of the crystals in a box she had found in an op shop a few months ago.

Stella knew she didn't have any ornate jars like the witches had in their workshop, but she did have a small vegemite jar she had been saving for something special. After checking whether the mirror still had the ingredients written on it—it didn't—she made a cuppa and sat at the bench. There were no measurements or directions, so Stella lined up all the ingredients.

Into the jar, Stella placed the crystals. Next, she opened the chamomile and peppermint tea bags and sprinkled the contents of each on top of the crystals.

Opening the packet of cloves, she decided to place three cloves into the jar. Lastly, she crumbled and added one cinnamon stick.

Using some glitter paper left over from one of Andie's projects, she wrote down the ingredients and glued the paper on top of the jar.

"Is that fancy enough? Should I be adding anything else? Maybe I should say something, like a chant or a word spell?"

> *Money, abundance and prosperity,*
> *I call to thee.*
> *Come to me...*
> *So mote it be...*

Feeling lighter and more energetic, Stella placed the jar on the window sill. Time for a brisk walk around the block before darkness set in.

Putting her hands in the pockets of her coat as she put it on, Stella was hoping to find her lapis stone she misplaced a few weeks ago. She didn't find her crystal, but she unfolded a piece of paper she found tucked in neatly at the bottom.

"What is this?" The writing was tiny, neat and flowery. The paper was like parchment, or like the paper she had dyed with tea once, experimenting with different craft ideas.

"This looks very similar to the paper in the witch's book in my dream. Squinting, she read what was written on the scrap of paper.

> *Spell for abundance and prosperity:*
> *On a bay leaf, write the amount of money you need,*
> *Light the bay leaf, and burning the bay leaf, set your intention.*
> *Power of bay leaf, I ask thee,*
> *Through methods fair and just,*
> *Bring abundant prosperity.*
> *Through the fire,*
> *So mote it be.*

Stella had no idea how the piece of paper got into her pocket. The coat was one she had found in the wardrobe when she moved. While she wouldn't normally wear something that wasn't hers, it was purple, her favourite colour.

"How curious that it is another prosperity spell. Maybe it is just a coincidence.

"I don't suppose there is a bay leaf hiding in here anywhere, is there?" She smiled, feeling in the corners of the pockets. She added bay leaf to her shopping list on the fridge.

Old Friends

Luna

Luna looked through her wardrobe. She was missing her favourite coat. She hadn't worn it for years, but she distinctly remembered having a beautiful purple coat.

"Did I drop it into the second chance shop?" she wondered.

She knocked on the back of the wardrobe to see if the coat was somehow hiding where she couldn't see it.

"Whoa!" She jumped back, watching in amazement as the back of the wardrobe opened. A portal! In her wardrobe! This was not what she expected to find when she went looking for her coat.

Without hesitating, she walked through the portal. She looked around the dress shop she found herself in. It looked familiar.

"Well really!" She smiled. Although she couldn't see anyone, she was sure she had ended up in the United Kingdom in the seventeenth century. She grabbed what looked like her purple coat, hanging on the hook on the back of the wooden door, as she walked through the shop and out the door.

The street outside looked familiar. Luna remembered being here before. She pulled the coat around her as she strode down the cobbled street to the "Headless Woman" pub.

"Luna!" the publican shouted as she entered. "It's been too long."

"Catherine!" Luna grinned back, accepting the tankard of ale her friend handed to her. "It's quiet in here today."

"Well, it is Friday morning. Most people are at the markets," the bartender looked at her quizzically. "Why aren't you down there selling your herbs and spices?"

"It's been a long time since I have peddled my wares at the crossroads. Longer than we think." She took a long drink of the ale, then, looking at the tankard regretfully, she placed it back on the bar.

"By the way, the portal has opened again at Tizzies Dress Ups. The Coven might want to close it again before anyone else comes through. Or goes through," the crone told her fellow witch.

"That might be tough. We haven't met for a while now. Scattered far and wide. Too many were being tortured, and worse." Catherine shuddered.

Luna pulled herself up on the old wooden bar stool, as big and old and chunky as she remembered. "These were a great idea, sister."

"Why thank you. I tried to keep the place the same, in memory of all of us who have passed through these doors."

Looking around at the wooden beams on the ceiling and the walls, the low tables and chairs along the walls, the atmosphere was exactly as she remembered.

"Right, well we do need to close that portal, preferably when I am on the other side again, or my animals will miss me."

Leaning on the bar, Catherine asked, "Pets or children?"

"A cat, Salem and Maude, a magpie—Australia, over three hundred years." Luna shrugged. "I haven't seen the children in many years."

REACHING ACROSS THE bar, the friends embraced.

It had been a long time since these two had embraced in person. Their coven had worked with other magical folk to keep everyone safe. Making sacrifices. Witches, women with powers to heal, were shunned, bullied, victimised, imprisoned, or worse.

Holding her dear friend's hands, Luna spoke with affection and love.

"You have to stay safe, to keep the pub open for others who may pass through. I'll close the portal from the other side. It can be done." She hoped she sounded more positive than she felt.

"But Luna, by yourself, have you been practising?"

"Dribs and drabs, I fear I have been lazy, enjoying the peace and quiet in my world. This portal opened in my wardrobe while I was looking for this coat.

Which I found on this side of the portal. I don't know what that means. What I do know is this coat."

Luna reached into the pockets and pulled a book from the pocket on the right, "This coat has a habit of providing the added oomph needed for any spell.

"Last time I was here, it helped us escape. There is a magic in this coat, an old magic. It seems to know exactly what is needed in any situation."

"How will I know you are okay?"

"You won't. At least not until my next visit. I think you will only know if I am not."

The crone moved quickly, without looking back. If she had stayed with her friend any longer, she would have found it very difficult to leave.

LANDING IN THE BACK of her wardrobe, Luna grabbed the bag of protection herbs that she had discovered in the left side pocket of her coat and sprinkled it at the back of the wardrobe. She whispered the words in the Old English script in the notebook from so long ago. Hearing a zap, like an energy or electrical charge, she was satisfied that, for now, the portal was sealed and safe from intruders. She missed her friend terribly, but now was not the time for regrets.

Stella

Stella had been putting off the task of writing letters to her children. She wanted to tell them how much she loved them in writing in case anything ever happened to her before they all reconciled.

"Do it now," whispered her spirit guides. "Make it happen." Stella felt a zap, like the type of zap you feel when you put your finger on something electric and it shorts out. A pure electric charge. She jumped. Charged with a boost of positive energy, she wrote to each of her children, tucking the completed letters in the front of her scrapbook.

Luna

Luna walked around her garden, checking the plants, looking for signs of pests.

"These cooler autumn days are the perfect time to get out in the garden and tidy up the plants," Luna told the many little birds flitting around the bushes.

"I am so glad you little guys don't eat my figs, peaches and nectarines." Luna climbed up the rickety old ladder to grab the last of the fruit.

"That's enough exercise for the day." Luna picked up her old basket, full of the last harvest of fruit, carrots, broccoli, peppermint, basil, lavender and tarragon. She struggled with the basket, half carrying and half dragging it.

"It's a shame I can't harness you and have you drag this up the path for me," she said as Salem bounced and darted along beside her. He was getting older but had lost none of his playful streak, Luna decided, as the crazy kitten zigzagged around the basket and her feet.

As the sun started its slow descent into the evening sky of purple and pink, Luna stewed the last of the fruit, ready to eat during the Mabon feast the following day. Her old saucepan had held many such mixtures, soups, stews and potions.

"I bet you are almost as old as me," she whispered as she stirred the mixture. If the saucepan had been a colour other than silver, the remnants of that colour had long since worn away.

There is a subtle shift in the weather and the seasons as autumn sets in. There are fewer hours of daylight, the nights are longer. It is a time of inward reflection, a time to consider settling in and getting cosy, resting up after the long hot summer. The second of the harvest festivals, Mabon, the Autumn Equinox, is a time to collect and gather and save for the longer, colder winter months to come. We celebrate the foods we grow and store for the winter. We share our gathered foods, a shared celebration, or maybe we celebrate alone. The way of the witch. A time of thanksgiving for the bounty of the earth, reminding us it is time to prepare for winter. This sabbat is associated with balance and harmony, as day and night are once again of equal length. We honour the balance between light and dark within ourselves.

Luna read back through her notes written so long ago. She added to the notes from time to time. She found the page she had painstakingly created on her first Mabon celebration. Creating her witchy journal had taught her patience and attention to detail. These skills did not come easily, but over time, she had calmed down enough to create and celebrate.

Some activities to celebrate the Autumn equinox:

1. *Make a gratitude list; the equinox is a time to feel grateful for the*

harvest and to show gratitude for things in your life.
2. *Restore balance, especially at home. Have a clean-out and get rid of things you no longer use.*
3. *Tend a fire—burn and release old papers, leaves and garden waste.*
4. *Be creative.*
5. *Walk in nature.*
6. *Baking.*
7. *Planting seeds.*

"I have searched everywhere for my basil pesto recipe." Luna looked around her cottage exasperatedly. The cottage was cute and tiny. The only items the crone kept were books, herbs, crystals, candles and assorted other bits and pieces. Her one indulgence of her past life was the big old chest that doubled as a seat, a bench, a table or somewhere for Salem to sit in the early morning sun.

"Could it be in the chest? I really would prefer not to open that. Too many memories." She sighed.

"I don't want to waste all the basil I collected today. I am going to have to open it," the crone told Sherilee, the purple glass butterfly hanging above the chest. Every morning the sun shone through the beautifully coloured butterfly, giving the cottage a lovely purple hue.

"Help me find the recipe," she whispered to her friend.

As soon as she opened the chest, she saw the book. Her very first *Book of Spells.* The purple cover she had made from scraps of paper and material. She had even made some of the paper herself.

"I remember Tizzie helped me bind this together and stitch the pages in." Luna thought back to that time when she was still learning about the witch wheel of the year. She had struggled to remember what activities or correspondences were linked to each festival or celebration.

Tizzie and Catherine found her and guided her, tapping into the magic within herself. They had invited her to join their coven. She had spent hours writing things in her book to help her remember the activities that corresponded with each of the year's celebrations.

Fondly she flipped through the pages of the journal.

"I thought it was a good way of teaching myself to cook, to make and create things, like a real witch," she told Salem. He was watching her, loving the sound of her voice.

Some simple ideas for the harvest festivals
Traditional Harvest Fare can include:

- *A bowl of fruit*
- *Oven-roasted vegetables*
- *Baking sourdough bread*
- *Making Kombucha*
- *Basil pesto*
- *Pecan pie*
- *Harvesting garlic, onions, cucumber, carrots, and other vegetables to pickle and jar and store and keep the food gathered for the colder winter months*
- *Fermenting foods*
- *Making tinctures and infusions and medicinal herbals*
- *Freezing mint in ice cube trays*
- *Juicing and freezing*
- *Harvest celebrations can also be about making altar decorations*

"Perfect!" Startling Salem as she jumped to her feet, she bent down and scooped him up. "Come on Salem, time to make some pesto!"

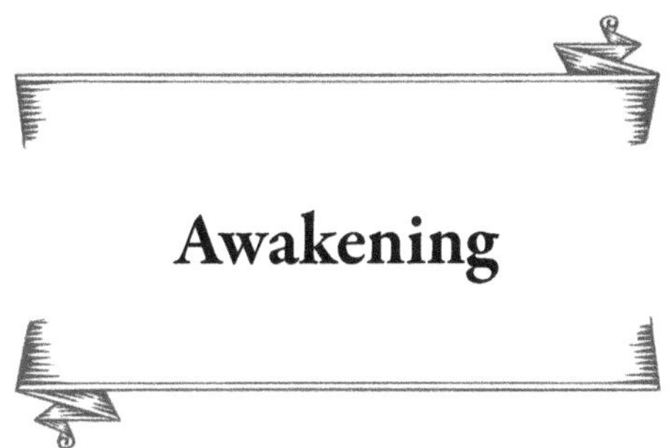

Awakening

S tella

Stella was torn between following her intuition and her fear of getting it wrong.

"What do I do?" she spoke out loud to no one in particular. She wanted to see if she was magic, whatever that meant. She just didn't know where to start. She didn't want to get it wrong.

"Follow your intuition," the voice spoke gently but firmly.

Stella jumped. "Now I am hearing things."

"Follow your intuition. You have the answers yourself," the voice was unmistakably real.

"What the?" Stella stood up, nearly knocking over her desk chair. This wasn't the first time she had heard the voice, her spirit guide gently coaxing her, but this was the loudest and firmest.

After carefully examining the house and finding no one and no secret microphones or recordings hidden anywhere, she settled back down at her desk.

"Okay then, I will follow my intuition."

With pen and paper at the ready, she composed her shopping list:

- *Book of Shadows (notebook)*
- *Pens and glitter etc to decorate Book of Shadows*
- *Birthday candles as spell candles—because all other candles take too long to burn out in one sitting*
- *A basil plant, olive oil, garlic, pine nuts and parmesan cheese for basil pesto*
- *Coloured ribbon and string*
- *A peppermint plant and oregano and thyme*

Stella wanted to start her witchy life by celebrating the autumn harvest festival.

"I think having grown up in Tumut, the town with the autumn festival of the falling leaf, this is a good place to start." She smiled to herself.

"I don't think I need anything else. I don't want to have to go back to the shop if I forget something." Stella amused herself, talking back to her guides as if they were right there with her.

"I should be able to get it all at the plaza, so I don't have to drive too far. I'll be back home in an hour." She grabbed the keys as she flew out the door.

An hour later and Stella had already put the plants in water in the kitchen sink and was sitting at the table decorating her little purple *Book of Spells*.

When all is said and done, there is nothing more to be said,

So be careful with words we can't take back,

And forgive those who knew no better and didn't intend any harm.

Harm no one, forgive trespasses, our own and others.

Love others, and above all, love and believe in ourselves, in our magic and our abilities for change, magic and miracles.

So mote it be.

Stella

"Does being a witch or a pagan mean I am no longer a Christian?" wondered Stella.

"It's Easter, and for the last thirty years at least, Easter has meant going to church. Do I still go to church this year? Do I want to? Do I have to?" Stella was curious.

"I am more interested in the pagan celebrations than Christian ones at the moment. I think I am evolving, thinking for myself more and not following rules that I have always followed.

"As far back as I can remember, as a child, and then as mum to my own children, I have attended at least one of the rituals that Catholic's celebrate over Easter."

This Easter, the children were all with their dad at their grandparent's home in rural NSW.

Stella realised this meant she didn't have to attend church over the Easter period at all. Unless she wanted to.

Did she want to?

She thought about this for a while.

"I do believe that Jesus and Mary were people who lived a very long time ago and influenced generations of people."

"I don't believe in a traditional male God, but in a goddess, as steward of the earth."

"I also believe in magic."

She sat with her thoughts for a while.

Stella was still very angry with her Catholic upbringing.

"I did everything that was expected, everything that was right, yet I lost my children. There has to be a better way. I don't know much about witchcraft, but this weekend seems like a good time to start."

"Trust yourself," whispered the spirits that seemed to be with Stella a lot these days.

"Listen."

As Stella looked around, she was sure she saw figures moving around. Just out of the corner of her vision. Nothing more than a blur.

She closed her eyes and quietened her breathing and her mind. Using her third eye, that spot in the middle of her forehead, to focus on the light. She could intuitively see—or sense—a bright white light. Opening her eyes and keeping her breathing steady, she followed the light, out the kitchen door, down the steps and to the back of the garden to the thick hedge.

The light seemed to pass straight through the hedge.

"How do I follow the light? How do I get through there? There is a main road on the other side," she tried to think logically. Her intuition told her something else.

Closing her eyes so that her brain didn't tell her that she was about to get covered in prickles and cut her hands, she pushed the hedge open and walked through. Using her other senses, it felt like she had pushed back a thick, velvety curtain.

When she opened her eyes, she was in a field. There were a couple of old wooden barns, not colour bond or metal sheds. These looked like they were hundreds of years old. There was a stone wall in the distance. She assumed it led along a road, although she couldn't see any people or cars. It didn't look like any farmland area near where she lived. It looked more like the English countryside she had seen on television.

Bending down to examine the grass, it was a weird weedy, tumbly plant she didn't recognise. It was green but also brown, and some parts of it were fluffy and thick. She turned to the closest row of trees. Not eucalypts or anything she immediately recognised. These trees were tall and wide, branches laden with green leaves. As she walked over to the trees, scenes flashed in front of her as if she was watching a movie. She didn't recognise any of the people or the places. Feeling dizzy, Stella sat down at the base of the tree to catch her breath.

STELLA WOKE UP AND looked around her. She was in her bed, in her purple flannel pyjamas. The room was dark. Her hair was still tied up in the high ponytail on the top of her head. She was still wearing her socks. Normally at bedtime, she took off her socks and plaited her long dark hair to stop it tangling during the night. She looked out the window. Her curtains were open, but it was pitch black outside.

"The last thing I remember was sitting down at the base of a big tree." Suddenly wide awake, she sprung out of bed, closing the bedroom curtains, before turning on the kitchen light.

"Did I really walk through the hedge and end up in another land?" she mused. "And if so, where did I end up? Also, how did I get back home, in bed with pyjamas on?"

Sitting at the bench in the kitchen with her laptop and a cup of coffee, she typed "big old trees" into Google. Frowning at the result, she tried "fluffy, tumbly grass", which made no sense even as she typed it.

"It's one in the morning!" Stella exclaimed, glancing up at the clock on the microwave. "No wonder I am feeling hungry." She spied half a loaf of bread left from Emily and Andie's visit on Monday. Absent-mindedly grabbing the tub of margarine from the fridge, she glanced at the postcard of the Scottish Highlands from her librarian friend Mrs K on her trip to Scotland for her mother's funeral. The postcard was a picture of stone walls along the roadside, fluffy grass, and tall trees that looked like they were hundreds of years old.

"Did I dream it all?" It certainly was starting to feel like a dream.

"Did I just fall asleep and dream about this postcard?"

She remembered thinking about Easter, church and being a witch. Following a light down the backyard and walking through the hedge.

"Am I going mad?"

"Do I go back down to the hedge now and see if I can walk back through it?" Stella laughed to herself at how crazy those words sounded. Looking out the window at how dark it was, she decided not to go back out in the dark to investigate further.

"If it was a full moon, or if there were street lights, I would venture out again, maybe. Tomorrow though, I am definitely checking it out again."

As Stella climbed back into her bed, snuggling down under the lilac quilt cover, she smiled. Shades of purple always made her happy. She had chosen the lighter coloured bed covering to lighten the room, donating the darker blue cover to the rag bag.

She was pleased with her internet search. She had found that the weird grass was likely to be gorse or heather, and the trees were most likely Scots Pine. These were common in Scotland, in particular the Scottish highlands. Closing her eyes, her dreams were filled with dancing in the Scottish fields, under big trees with fairies, elves and other magical creatures.

Luna

Luna had discovered witchcraft accidentally.

She loved crystals, candles, essential oils and plants. She and her children had spent hours collecting and using crystals and rocks, herbs and flowers. Luna remembered that time fondly. The innocence of learning and playing with her children. Their little faces beaming as she showed them the power of healing with lavender, with peppermint, and how rose quartz helped to calm and quieten their emotions. All four of her children had shown a remarkable aptitude for gardening and creating artworks using natural dyes. Those were the best times.

When Catherine and Tizzie found Luna through a portal in her dreams. Luna wondered if she would have lost her children if she hadn't helped them.

"If I had refused to help Catherine and Tizzie to close the portals, and magic had wiped out the non-magical people, I would have probably lost them anyway." Luna was out in the garden, pruning back the prickliest hedge of citrus trees. She had let the oranges and mandarins grow too closely together, and now it was a challenge to collect the fruit before it spoilt.

"So magic found me." Luna savagely chopped large sections of the trees to give them a chance to breathe, competing with each other for sunlight and water. "The thing is, I think I would still help them if I had the chance again. But I would make sure the kids were protected."

When her children were taken away, she had started drinking heavily.

"Luckily Catherine and Tizzie saw what was happening and drew me back to magic, allowing me to heal."

She loved becoming one with nature, the rituals, the celebrations, the spells and chants to the various goddesses. These activities linked her to the witches and magic folk from across centuries, and she loved that connection.

Letters to Stella's Children

To you all, my beautiful precious children.

I can't change the past. No matter how much I wish I had more confidence as a parent, as your mother. I can't go back and decide to stay and tell your dad to leave with such authority that he does. I can't go back and demand Christmases with you, or demand that you spend time with me. I always thought by being me and giving you space and time and opportunity that you would choose to come back to me.

Your dad was the fun parent, the one you all wanted to spend time with. I yearned for more time with you, I cried and sobbed for more time with you, but I wasn't strong enough to demand or fight. I will forever regret that.

I can't change the way you think or feel or the experiences of your childhood. I still yearn for time with you, with each of you. I want to know all about you, how you are going, what life is like for you. I can't make you want to spend time with me, not even just for a lunch. I could travel halfway around the world, but if you say no, I have to accept that. I still don't have the confidence as your mother to demand or expect it.

I will never give up though. I will always walk past your photo and say hello, good morning, how is your day? I hope everything is okay. I will still have dreams where we have a better relationship. I will still write out birthday cards every year for you.

I will forever hold on to the hope that one day I will answer the phone and hear your voice. Open my emails and read your email, or open the door to see you standing there. Whether you are thirty, fifty, or any age, you will always be my child, and you will always be welcome. I can't change what you feel or believe, but I can dream for that future where we connect again, like we did when you were oh so small.

<u>Pedro – my firstborn</u>

My beautiful little boy, you were born by caesarean. I had been suffering pre-eclampsia (pregnancy high blood pressure). Every June, there was a June long weekend celebration just for you. My perfect little boy. You may have been tiny, but you grew just perfectly, hitting every milestone as expected, or earlier than average. I had no idea what I was doing; I just knew I loved my little boy so much and wanted to do everything right for you. You had awful colic and didn't sleep much at all, so there were many nights snuggled together to calm you down. You will always be one of the very best things in my life, you and your three beautiful sisters.

From combat crawling to crawling and walking, all before you turned one year old, my inquisitive and clever boy was soon talking, being creative—painting, playdough, drawing, reading (you loved books, and we read all day long), playing cards like memory, and all types of games. We played outside on the swings, went for long walks, gardened, cooked. We were inseparable. You doted on Dad as well, and followed him around. When we disagreed, me and your dad, you would crawl between us, trying to fix whatever was wrong.

I had no great family memories of bonding when I was growing up, and I was determined to do it differently. As your mother, I wanted to give you all the things as a family that I missed out on. I wanted you to have a calm and happy family, and I did whatever I could to make it happen. I loved playing with you and teaching you. I loved sewing and knitting, making clothes and toys for you.

When you were little, you and I spent every day together. We went to the park, we played with all your toys and puzzles, and you had heaps—as our first and precious baby boy, we bought you all manner of puzzles, toys, planes, cars, books, blocks and games. We watched television and videos, one of your favourite shows was Noddy. Another was Thomas the Tank Engine. Play School was another favourite show we watched together. The Wiggles formed as a band the year you were born.

We went to church, and after church, we went to visit family every Sunday morning until they moved to Tindal when you were around one year old. You could speak and read and write and tell the time by the time you were three. You loved each of your sisters as they were born. You tried so hard to look after them, and they looked up to you.

When I was pregnant with your baby sister, you wanted a little brother called Andrew, understandable as you had two sisters already. So when she was born, we made her middle name Andrea. It was as close as we could get to giving you a brother.

Then the rift happened. Things were said, things were misheard and misunderstood. Stubbornness played a part. We didn't know how to reconnect. We believed what was said by others. I wasn't strong enough or mature enough to understand that I could have fought to stay in touch and keep in touch, despite everything else that was going on.

I never wanted you to choose not to stay with me. I made my decisions to keep each of my children safe. I kept asking how you were. I kept asking you to come and visit and come and live with me. I always wanted you and wanted to be a part of your life.

I will always regret not fighting for you. I will always hold on to the hope that one day you will forgive me, that one day we will reconnect. I will always believe that one day we will have a relationship, to be there for you, to hear all about your life, what makes you happy and sad, and how everything is going. I will always be here for you, right by your side.

All my love, now and forever.

Your mum x

KAY, MY FIRSTBORN PRINCESS daughter

My firstborn daughter, a dancer and go-getter, with your full head of dark hair, you were a little angel. I was so filled with love for you, little bundle of energy. Full of laughter and joy and a sense of mischief to match your brother's more placid personality. I loved our early morning walks to the park. You and your brother dressed in full-on parka gear and gumboots to side down the slide, and swing on the swings before settling in for a day of crafts, painting, reading and watching children's television. Life with you both was so much fun.

You loved playing uno, and memory, doing puzzles and painting. Bascially doing anything your brother did. You thought riding your scooter down the slippery dip was so much fun. Bedtime though, was not as much fun. I hated controlled crying. I didn't like seeing you crying yourself to sleep. You just didn't like the cot, as once you got into the big bed, you fell asleep straight away.

After the initial scare when you were born, you quickly grew into a cheeky little bundle of joy, willing to give everything a try. Like me, you loved chocolate and lollies, anything sweet. I didn't realise that your food allergies could have been worked on, but no regrets, I just hope you are happy and content and well and doing what you love.

You grew up so fast. One minute you were this cute little bundle of joy following right behind your big brother, trying to keep up, the next, you were all grown up, going after your life, study and career dreams. When you were little, you were friends to everyone, not shy at all. You would talk to anyone, adult or child, with such enthusiasm and so full of energy. You made friends easily, with Chelsea across the road, with Tanya and with boys and girls at preschool, school, dancing, always talking, always on the go.

You always wanted to help. You were right there, mothering everyone, looking after everyone. You never sat still. It was tough on you when I left and divorced Dad. I honestly thought it was the best thing for you and your brother and sisters. I may have made many mistakes in my life, but when it came to you, each and every decision I made, I thought they were the best at the time.

My dancer, and little princess, I am so proud of you. Love you so much. You were so talented with your dancing, and so dedicated, and so wanted to succeed, achieve and excel, at dancing, at school, and at everything you did. Jazz dancing, tap dancing, ballet, you were willing to try anything. Basketball, soccer, competition bicycle riding. You went after your dreams, and you achieved everything you put your mind to.

You were so little when you won the competition at Riverside. I will never forget how proud I was of you. I am proud of you. I was so proud when you were working with Lizzie. She thought the world of you, as do I. You are such a brave girl. In hospital getting your teeth out, when you entered the competition where we met Lizzie, at school and at university, moving house and changing jobs and in your relationships. You give everything you do one hundred percent. You try and excel, and people love and respect you for it. I am very proud of you, always have been and always will be.

You took on the role of looking after your sisters, and you tried hard to help everyone. I love your kind soul and spirit.

I wish I could have protected you and kept you safe. That's all I ever wanted to do.

I look forward to the day when we connect again, as I so want to have a relationship with you as you grow and mature, to be there for you, to hear all about your life, what makes you happy and sad, and how everything is going. I will always be here for you, right by your side.

All my love, now and forever.

Mum xxx

<u>Emily, to my quiet empath</u>

The fun continued with my beautiful young gymnast. Quiet and placid compared to your siblings, you would do things like fall asleep in the high chair or slip out of the pram as we crossed the road. Happy to tag along to preschool. Big brother went, big sister loved it and you wanted to go too, so you joined in from day one. You were happy to be with us, quiet, unassuming, brightening everyone's day with your smile. You did things the others didn't try, like crawling up the aisle when I was reading in church or discovering that big brother's birthday party was a great opportunity to eat all the food left over when the kids went out to play.

I cherish every memory of our time together when you were growing up. It was a rocky, tumultuous time for you, the breakup and divorce hit you as much as the older two, yet you were so quiet, you never made a fuss. From the day you were born, you were this quiet, smiling, peaceful child who seemed happy to wait your turn. I know how tough it was in a family where everyone else was noisy and yelling and competing. My memories of you are as a beautiful, petite, sweet, kind and caring sister, daughter and friend. You were keen to try every sport, and you excelled at most of them, netball, football, basketball, little athletics, aerobics, circle skills and, of course, gymnastics.

My gorgeous gymnast, how proud I am of you, now and always. You tried your best, competing in rhythmic gymnastics across the state, loving it but also putting very high expectations on yourself.

When you were born, my gorgeous strawberry blonde princess, the only one of four siblings whose birth was normal and without drama. You happily lay in your cradle, babbling happily while I fed and changed your older brother and sister, rarely raising your voice. You were so cute, every single thing you did was so precious... your smile did and still does light up a room!

I want you to always know and remember how much I love you, how proud I am of you, and how much I cherish who you are and our friendship over the years. Much quieter than the others, you had a few close friends, and you are kind and friendly to everyone you meet. You give everyone a chance. You are such a clever girl at everything you try. You never gave up, but persisted in whatever you set your mind to. I always admired your tenacity, your poise, your determination and your abilities.

You found things tough, but you worked through it yourself, not bothering me with anything. I wish I had been more receptive to that. I wish I had spent more time helping you discover the world around you, find a safe place to be, and learn and grow. I didn't realise the stress and anxiety you went through because you kept it all to yourself, not wanting to bother me.

I love and cherish the time together when you were growing up, and the time we spend together now we are both adults and interested in many of the same things. You are wise beyond your years. So many experiences have made you the wonderful woman you are today. Your love of travel, learning new things and trying new foods, your university study, you pack so much into your life, making the most of every single day. I love spending time with you and talking to you on the telephone.

You are my awesome gorgeous beautiful empath, and always will be.

All my love now and forever,

Mum xx

<u>Andie, my miracle child</u>

Birth number four was certainly a different way to enter the world. We didn't think our beautiful girl would survive the night, given only a thirty per cent chance. But you defied the odds, and with no long-term side effects at all. Hospital for five weeks, some of that in an induced coma, and then another five weeks at home on oxygen. Such a roller coaster, such tenacity and drive, coupled with kindness and love. Despite family jokes, you were always wanted and loved.

I want you to know how much I love you, how proud I am of you and how much I cherish your friendship. Despite your rough start, and rocky family life, you are a kind, loving, caring, clever, bright, intelligent and loyal daughter, friend, sister and human being. You worked extremely hard, at school, at work and at university. You worked just as hard at your friendships and family friendships. You are the one who tries to keep all your siblings on track, the one who looks after your dad and also still has time for your close friends and me.

I cherish the memories of our time together when you were growing up. We watched crime shows on Tuesday nights and Saturday nights. When you were little, we used to come home and watch your favourite characters in other television shows or videos. You and your siblings loved movie night with videos and junk food, and of course sleepovers with friends.

You helped so much at work in childcare. At three years old, you helped us with the other kids, always greeted the parents with a smile, and helped set up the activities and pack up afterwards. Even at a very young age you were cooking (chicken in foil in a microwave doesn't work so well), you helped cook dinners, cakes and muffins. You and your friends made the most awesome (awful) concoctions for us to eat. You had so much fun with your friends, and of course, you were the most awesome little big sister to your nearly-step little brother. You had close friends at crèche, and you have enjoyed close friends ever since. You are a happy, smiling, genuine person who everyone loves to be around.

You always had this way of pushing through your anxiety and getting it done. Whether it was packing for Dad's house, learning to read, or playing basketball. I wish I had helped more with your anxiety, that I had spent more time with you as you navigated the world.

You are the baby of the family and, in many ways, the most mature from a very young age. I know one of the stories in the family is that I didn't want you, but that is very far from the truth. You were just as wanted and loved as your three siblings. Your brother dearly wanted a little brother called Andrew, and that's why your middle name is Andrea. Your brother and sisters loved and doted on you. They were so worried when you were in hospital as we all were. They were at the hospital to help the lovely nurses give you your first bath once you were awake from your coma. It was interesting factoring in an oxygen bottle at bath time and change time, and it was heavy when I dropped it on my foot... Luckily that only happened once.

I love spending time with you now, as an adult, as well as when you were younger. We may not see each other often, but we do have fun when we get together.

So many more things to say, so much more time to be spent with you. I cherish every single moment and every single memory.

You are my awesome gorgeous special beautiful 'baby' girl. Always will be.

All my love now and forever,

Mum xx

<u>Other things I should have said to my children.</u>

Our identities are an eclectic mix of all sides of our families. All mixed up and connected. It is why we connect more with some people in our families than others. We are shaped by our families, our environment and a shared history. You were each fortunate to have spent time with your dad's side of the family, your grandparents, aunts, uncles and cousins. Unfortunately, you didn't get to meet or spend time with my mum or dad or much time with my sister or family on my mum's side of the family. It seems like such a long time ago. There is a whole lot of family history information at home about our side of the family, and some pictures, etc., too, if / when you ever want to know more about our side of the family.

My wish for you is for you to know that you have always been more than enough, that you are truly special people because you were born and because you are loved.

<u>The journey</u>

Did you know that life is a journey and that we don't have to know the ending yet?

You don't have to be perfect, achieve the highest grades, or be the best at anything. Being you is enough. Just as you are.

Did you know you can change your mind multiple times? You don't have to always know the answer or always get it right?

You can choose a different path, to travel or move or learn something new no matter how old you are.

You don't have to know all the answers now or ever.

You don't need to know the end destination. You can have fun on every step of the journey.

Did you know that you can be happy, have fun, and dance and sing if you want to?

You don't have to be serious all the time.

Being stubborn and independent can be assets, but they can also be the worst traits if we miss opportunities for connection, forgiveness and fun.

We can all make mistakes and be forgiven and try again.

Pets can be great friends and companions.

Wish upon a star every chance you get.

Op shops and recycling things are okay.

Traveling somewhere new can heal and soothe the soul.
It is okay to be alone; we don't need another person to make us whole.
It is okay to forgive other people, and important to forgive ourselves.
It is okay to say no.

We never stop loving our family, even when we are apart or aren't connected.

Friends can be family, and family can be friends.

Letting go of anger, pain and regret is a healthy way of living.

Take a chance on something that is important.

Kindness is a way of life, so is gratitude.

There is no perfect time to make a start on something; it is best just to make a start.

Crying and showing emotions is okay.

Sometimes things are sad and can't be fixed or mended.

Things change, but change isn't always scary.

Balance, harmony, being grounded are skills we can all learn.

We can follow our intuition.

We don't always have to struggle. Life can be good; we just have to believe in ourselves.

These are just some of the things I wish I had taught you or told you when you were younger.

Love always,

Mum xx

Past, Present and Future

Hindsight is a wonderful thing, said in sarcasm. Moving forward, one step at a time. Owning who we are. Acknowledging those who matter.

Luna

"I do wish I could have said and done things differently. But then, I guess I wouldn't be here, and I do love this place. Everything happens for a reason. I know magic is real. If I remember to be positive and set clear intentions, anything is possible. Until I know what is next, I will keep working in the garden, practising spells, making herbal potions and lotions, healing and releasing, preparing for whatever the future brings."

Stella

Stella was also feeling positive.

She poked and prodded the hedge, trying to get through as she did the day before. Today it seemed like a hedge, nothing more complicated or magical. She threw the spade she was holding in frustration.

"What do I do now?" she asked the magpie looking at her quizzically.

"I don't think I dreamt it. I didn't drink any alcohol yesterday."

"Would it be a portal?" she asked the bird, not expecting an answer. Stella wasn't even sure what a portal was. The idea of a magical door in her hedge, with the main road behind it, that somehow took her into a land many thousands of miles away sounded nonsensical.

"What do I need to know about portals? How do I find out?" She looked up and saw three magpies sitting on the large tree by the hedge. They held her stare before flying up over the house, over the telephone line.

"I feel like they were trying to tell me something, but what?" she placed the spade back into the garden bed closest to the hedge. "The only thing in the direction the birds went is the telephone line."

"Unless it is the internet," While the internet wasn't the perfect research tool, Stella didn't own any books on magic, and she figured that she had to start somewhere. She ran inside, made a cup of coffee and settled down to learn as much as she could.

Most of what she found on the internet were instructions for finding and using magic portals in various online video games. There was information about magic portals in stories, movies and books too. She was unable to find anything specific about opening magic portals in real life.

The entire time she was searching, she heard her guides whispering.
"Trust yourself."
"Believe in you."

Closing her laptop, she went back over the events of the day before. She remembered closing her eyes, following a light to the hedge. With her eyes shut, she had moved through to the other side.
"Is it that easy?" she wondered.

STELLA FORCED HERSELF to walk slowly past the pots of pink and yellow daisies and the peppermint and lavender in tubs at the end of the path. She loved herbs, their smell and healing properties. Reaching the hedge, she closed her eyes. Holding her hands in front of her, she felt the hedge and parted it, soft like velvet curtains.

When she opened her eyes, there were no fields or barns.

This time Stella found herself in an alleyway. Considering the style of the buildings and the clothing on the people scurrying by, she was probably in a market town, and it was probably hundreds of years ago. The cobbled stone path. The wooden buildings and doors, small and dark, entries into the various shops along the road. She could hear horse-drawn carriages on the main road. People scurried past, heads down, dressed in dark-coloured robes. Looking down at her clothes, black jeans and boots, with a long purple cardigan over her blue shirt, she hoped she wouldn't draw too much attention to herself.

Looking for a landmark to identify where the portal was, she saw a row of doors. The red door stood out amongst four black doors.

"Too obvious," she thought.

Studying the four black doors. She noticed that of the four doors, one looked considerably older than the rest. It was at the very end of the row, tucked away into the stone wall that seemed to go on forever.

"That one," she thought, memorising the way the door seemed to fade into the stone.

Before she could talk herself out of it, she marched off down the street to investigate.

AS STELLA WALKED AROUND the corner, she watched lots of people walking in both directions along the street in silence. Eyes averted, so as not to attract any glances from anyone else.

Further along the street, she could see the market, not too unlike markets back home.

Stallholders manned food stalls, strange smells of meats cooking that Stella didn't recognise, bundles of meat stuffs, vegetables and herbs hanging on hooks at the stalls. Stalls with bread and other baked goods in baskets at the front, the aromas tantalising passers-by. There were clothing stalls with racks of flowing robes, long shirts, undergarments and assorted clothing, belts and boots too. Other stalls featuring leather products, others with harnesses, leads and collars for horses, some stalls with woven baskets and hessian bags, wooden furniture, wooden wheels for buggies and wagons, stalls with tools with a strange array of products.

Stella was intrigued by everything she saw. Rows of semi-detached buildings. Some of them looked like homes; others were workplaces, with names above the doors, jewellers, bookstores, several taverns, and others.

As well as the noise created by the market stall owners, and the noise of the carriages and the horses, there was yelling. The crowd of people that were yelling were moving closer to where she was. Not entirely comfortable with all the commotion, she ducked into a doorway of a tavern, watching the crowd pass by in the middle of the road.

"You are not from around here," Stella jumped as a woman collecting glasses spoke to her.

"No, I'm not," Stella wasn't sure what else to say.

"Don't let the crowd scare you. The younger ones are always rowdy on market days." She smiled. "So what are you drinking?"

Stella wasn't sure how to answer. She wasn't entirely sure what time of the day it was, and she thought it was probably time to start thinking about going home. "Do you have coffee?"

"Coffee with a little dram of something to warm the soul?"

"I don't have any money, I mean, I didn't plan on coming in here," Stella wasn't quite sure what would happen next; she didn't just want to turn around and leave.

"Luckily the first drink is free!" beamed the woman.

Stella took the tankard and slid onto a stool at the bar. She was enjoying the atmosphere and the company of her new friend. She took a long sip of the drink.

"This is the best coffee!"

Just as she was about to engage the landlady in further conversation, a huge clap of thunder rattled the windows. Stella jumped.

"I'm Brigid, I own this auspicious establishment," with a flourish, "and you are welcome here anytime you pass by." She paused as another thunderclap quickly followed the first.

"Stella, and thank you, that would be great, although I don't know when I will be passing through here again. I think I should be heading home before the storm hits."

"I think I will be seeing you again soon." Brigid smiled knowingly. "But for now, yes, go home. We can talk more next time."

With a quick wave goodbye, Stella ducked out of the tavern and hurried back down the road. A crowd of people from the market was also hurrying past, likely on their way to shelter before the storm. Finding the alley with the red door, she moved quickly to the little door on the end. Looking for the door handle, she could feel the panic rising.

"Close your eyes." Not sure where the voice was coming from, she nevertheless followed the suggestion and closed her eyes.

Placing her hands where she felt the door handle should be, she felt a notch in the wood. She heard a tiny 'click' and felt the door move. She passed through the doorway.

Tentatively opening her eyes, she was looking at her house, and it was raining. Marvelling at what had just happened, she ran up the back steps, already saturated by the giant-sized raindrops.

The Storm

Luna

Luna watched the storm through the trees from inside her cottage. She didn't mind storms, but sometimes the storms seemed to come from a darker place. Tonight's storm had that ominous feeling. The huge claps of thunder and sheets of lightning were kilometres away and moving away from her cottage. She didn't feel threatened by the weather at all. It was more a feeling and a memory of times past.

"Do you think it is just a storm, or is there a new challenge ahead?" Salem looked at the crone with love but didn't answer her. Purring, he watched the storm from the safest place possible, snuggled in her lap.

From the moment she fell through that portal in the back of her wardrobe, she had been expecting trouble of some kind. She was cautiously satisfied that the storm was only a storm. And yet, she couldn't shake the feeling that this storm was the start of something big. Flooding in the village nearby would be devastating. Magic spilling over from other realms could be catastrophic.

Stella

Stella couldn't settle down to sleep.

"I travelled through a portal into another world!"

"HOW OFTEN CAN I TRAVEL back and forth? Is there a time limit? Also, will I always end up somewhere different?"

She wished there was someone she could ask. She had so many questions and no answers.

"Believe in you," whispered the voices, her guides.

"I would like to, but I don't know what I don't know," she responded.

"You will remember," the guides responded.

"I am pretty sure if I knew something like this, I wouldn't have forgotten, no matter how stressed my life has been!" Stella replied.

"Past, present, future, it's not linear, it is cyclical." She concentrated as they continued, "You have been there in a previous lifetime." This time, Stella was sure she caught a glimpse of a woman speaking.

Stella thought about it for a few minutes. Both her dreams and the place she visited through the hedge had seemed vaguely familiar. It was more of a feeling she couldn't shake that she had been there before. Could she have lived in the medieval town, been part of a coven, in another lifetime?

"Are both places linked? The forest and the coven and the medieval town?" she asked aloud.

Stella waited for a response from her guides.

Silence.

"Is the dream more than just a dream? Am I somehow visiting the past, or the future?"

Still no comments from her guides. Did that mean she was on the right track?

Too excited to sleep, Stella grabbed her phone and tucked it in the pocket of her cardigan. Maybe there would be the chance to take some photos, as long as she could take photos without arousing curiosity.

As she reached the hedge, she closed her eyes.

Opening her eyes, she was again in the same alleyway. It was dark. There was loud music and singing as she walked out of the alleyway. Revellers in the street, singing, raising their tankards in toasts to king and country. She slipped past one group, entering the tavern where she met Brigid, hoping to see her friend again. Brigid was busy filling tankards for customers. Stella couldn't catch her eye.

She slipped back out past the many people spilling in and out of the tavern and others like it along the cobblestone path.

Using instinct alone, Stella kept walking until the buildings dwindled, giving way to farmland, with occasional barns and farmhouses.

"Does this look the same as the first time I came through the hedge?" Stella wondered. "I suppose all farmland areas look the same." Although it was dark, she kept walking.

Five minutes later, she found herself in a forest. She wondered whether it was the same one from her dream. She closed her eyes, standing still, listening to the forest noises. She could hear an owl in the distance. She felt herself being pulled to the right, so she opened her eyes and moved in that direction.

Stella knew she should have been keeping track of where she had walked so that she could find her way home. Instead, she was fascinated by the size of the tall trees and the other plants and grasses that were so different from the plants she was used to at home. Some trees were straight and tall, reaching all the way up into the night sky. Others had branches that sprawled over a span of at least two metres. Even in the dark, with the overcast sky, she could see enough with the light of the moon to walk steadily and not trip on the many rocks and bushes scattered around the floor of the forest.

Not exactly following a path, more following a feeling or an energy. Soon she heard the familiar sound of chanting. As she came around into the clearing, she saw the three women, the witches from her dreams. The women stopped their chant as she got closer.

"Come and join us," the woman with the long plaits beckoned to her. "We are gathering plants and herbs. Those plants that need to be picked in the moonlight, after the rains."

"Are these some of the plants you use in your spell jars?" Stella asked.

"Yes, in spell jars, and lotions, and potions and tinctures, infusions, teas, even in cooking," the witch with the blonde hair replied.

"I'm Tizzie," the red-haired witch handed Stella a basket, "my friends, Luna," pointing to the witch with the plaits, "and Catherine," the witch with the blonde hair.

"Stella," Stella replied as she took the basket from her new friend.

An hour later, having collected mugwort, wormwood, burdock and assorted other plants, the witches invited Stella for a cup of tea. She happily followed them, enjoying the company of these ladies. So engrossed in talking with her new friends, she had completely forgotten she was supposed to be keeping an eye out for landmarks to help her get back to the portal, back home.

Luna

The storm seemed to have stopped as quickly as it started.

"That's a shame," she thought. "We could have done with more rain."

The crone was pleased that it appeared the storm had been ordinary and not something to be concerned about. Years ago, another similar storm had caught Luna and her coven unawares.

That storm had started a war between magical and non-magical folk, and had lasted years. She had been so immersed in learning magic to save her community that she had missed the signs that had led to her children being taken. Days of thunder and lightning, torrential rain, and a darkness that descended over their village and most of Scotland.

People were only just recovering from the crippling famine. The war between Scotland and England was in its early stages. Passion and patriotism were running high amongst all groups. It had taken Luna and her coven months to get the magical folk to safety and then close the portals.

When she had returned home, as mother, not crone, she had been devastated to find her children had vanished. No one knew where they had gone, who with, or why. Even with her magical resources, she couldn't find them.

Shaking off the feelings that always came over her when she thought back over those days, she reminded herself that some things were outside of her control.

"Thankfully the storm was just a storm," Luna said to Maude, who was patiently waiting at the door to say goodnight.

"Goodnight, my friend."

Halloween

Stella

The sound of her alarm woke Stella. Rubbing her eyes, she tried to remember how she got home.

"Were my new friends real? Or was it just a dream?"

"The last thing I remember was sitting around a small cast iron pot belly stove, sharing a pot of herbal tea."

"Luna—long plaits, Tizzie—blonde and Catherine—red hair," Stella said aloud so she would remember them. "Oh, and Brigid, the bartender."

Wishing it was the weekend so she could go back through the hedge, Stella went to work, counting down the hours until she could return to her friends.

Luna

Something was niggling in the back of her mind. There was something she had forgotten. Maude was fed and Salem was asleep in the sun on the front verandah. All her chores were done in the garden and the cottage for the day.

"There is something I am missing."

Her guides whispered, "Remember, past, present, future,"

They led her to her *Book of Spells* from her time in Scotland. Her journal was full of the many spells and correspondences, the directions for casting protection spells, for closing portals, for balancing the energies. She had scribbled down reams of information about what happened, what Catherine and Tizzie had taught her, and how to bring the people to safety and close the portals.

That storm had started on the eve of the Samhain, Halloween.

"It had been brewing since midsummer, but the witches had not noticed it straight away." She told Salem, "The thunder and lightning had lasted for days, the torrential rain with it. The clouds had been an eerie grey-green colour."

Flipping back a few days in the book, she found the entry about a new portal having appeared in the back of the dress shop. That same portal that Luna had walked through a few days ago, that had opened in the back of her wardrobe.

"So if that portal opened again recently, are other portals opening too?" Salem looked up from his position in the sun.

"If other portals are opening, what does it mean? Will they need me again, or are there others to take our place?"

"Is it such a bad thing if the portals open and magic returns? Others can sort it out."

As she closed the book, she noted the date—Samhain, Halloween, in Scotland, was the end of October. In Australia, it was the end of April. It took Luna a couple of seconds to realise the date.

"Today is Halloween!"

SAMHAIN, ALL HALLOWS Eve, or Halloween is on April 30 at sundown. The veil between the earth and the underworld thins. Spirits or ghosts may be more active. We can more easily communicate with those who have passed. It is a time to celebrate and give thanks for the bounty of the earth, the last harvests of the summer and to prepare for winter. A time to honour our ancestors. We acknowledge where we came from, our traits, and our gifts. A time to believe in the unexpected, in miracles and magic. We gather the last of the fruit and vegetables, pickle or store them, make bread and wine and save them for the celebrations to come.

"Even I get confused with Halloween in April," Luna said as she fed Maude her morning seed mix. "The veil is thinner now, here in Australia, but it is thinner in October overseas. Or maybe it is thinner at both places at the same time," Luna mused.

Maude finished her breakfast, bowed as was her custom, and flew away for her adventures.

Luna spoke to no one in particular, trusting her guides would answer her.

"If anyone can clarify what is happening, or if I am needed to help through the portal, I am listening."

The whispers began even before she had finished speaking. This had become customary, over the last thirty years, that all manner of spirits would whisper ideas and share knowledge with her. Listening to the voices, she learned so much about gardening, spells, witchcraft and folklore.

The whisperings didn't provide any more certainty on whether the portals were opening, and if they were, whether that would cause problems.

"Before I forget, it is time to honour those gone before, then we can garden."

LUNA'S SAMHAIN ALTAR was a simple affair. Photos of family and friends that she had loved and lost over the years. Lighting an altar candle and some incense, she gave thanks to each of them for having enriched her life. Feeling the old anxiety and pains bubbling to the surface, she hurried outside.

In the garden, every feeling, every thought and emotion could be planted and nurtured or weeded out, if necessary.

"A weed is just a plant growing in the wrong place. Like the dandelions. See here Salem, if I move the dandelions from the strawberry patch to this other bed under the citrus, they become perfectly respectable medicinal herbs."

Stella

Stella didn't yet know that the end of April was Halloween in the southern hemisphere.

Normally she loved spending time teaching the children in her class. Today though, she wanted the day over, so she could listen to the voices of the spirits of her ancestors. She wanted to walk through the hedge; she wanted to find her new friends, and she wanted to be a part of a coven.

"Hey Mum, what's for afternoon tea?" Andie bounced in just as Stella was about to head back down to the hedge.

"Andie! Did I forget to pick you up?" Stella couldn't believe she had been so distracted she had forgotten to pick up her daughter.

"NAH, I DECIDED TO COME and spend some time with you. Emily will pick me up after she finishes work." Andie opened the cupboard. "Do you want to make me pancakes?"

Stella gave her daughter a huge big bear hug. "Let's make them together."

Hours later, after she had spent the best afternoon, not just with Andie but with Emily as well, she waved to them as they drove away.

"Is it too late to go through the hedge?" she wondered.

"Should I try to meet up with them in my dreams instead?"

As she was trying to decide, two things happened.

She was absent-mindedly scrolling through a webpage describing the witch wheel in the southern hemisphere and discovered that today was Halloween in Australia.

Then she heard her guides.

"Be patient, there is time."

"Don't try too hard. It will work as it is meant to."

"That doesn't help at all," she whispered back.

Stella thought about what she had just read.

"Halloween in April, in autumn, does kind of make sense."

"A time to honour my ancestors," she read through her notes, "and the last harvest."

CLEARING A SPACE ON her desk, Stella lit a couple of tea-light candles. She found some photos of her parents, grandparents and other departed family. For those ancestors that she had no photos of, she wrote out their names. Scrounging around in the top drawer, she found some incense sticks. She lit one and placed it on the desk too. Next, she lined up all the crystals she had in front of the photos.

Stella was beginning to make sense of how ritual and talismans helped with focus and spellcraft.

"I don't know whether my ancestors were witches. There isn't anyone I can ask, but I would love to know if I have inherited this, whatever this is."

"And will my kids have similar experiences?"

"Take it slowly," they whispered.

Suddenly Stella felt exhausted. Deciding not to go through the hedge, she put on her purple pyjamas, and crawled into bed. Her last thought before falling asleep was of dancing in the forest with the three witches and the bartender.

Broomhilda – The Fairy

Broomhilda

The storm that was brewing this Halloween was in fact very similar to the storm on that other Halloween many years ago. Twenty-seven years ago, to be exact. Every twenty-seven years, a magical storm brews across all the realms. Mostly these storms bubble and boil and fizz out without developing any further.

Occasionally though, the storm awakens a magic deep within one of the realms.

Neither Luna nor Stella were fully aware of the depth of the magic they were connected to.

In each realm, there were magical folk who helped keep their world in balance. There were people from magical families who were stewards of their world, with a responsibility to keep magic in balance.

Broomhilda was from one of these families. For many generations, she had worked quietly out of sight to ensure people everywhere were safe from malevolent magic.

When magic surged, every twenty-seven years, she and others like her were normally able to calm the anomaly.

"Most of the time, I can manage it," Broomhilda said as she watched the latest storm brewing. The storm clouds held that eerie green hue, indicating that there was malevolent magic in one of the realms. A group of magical beings intent on causing trouble, collecting magic for evil intent. The strength of the storm confirmed there was a person whose magical power was developing who would assist in restoring the balance.

Luna and Stella were part of a family that had been blessed with magical powers centuries ago. The magic was stronger in some generations than others.

In some cases, it skipped a whole generation, growing stronger in the next. Luna was one to whom the magic had been bestowed. Stella was also one of the lucky ones. Having skipped a couple of generations, the magic had settled on her, lying dormant until she was ready.

Broomhilda had, from time to time, visited both as maiden, mother and crone.

"Being less than twenty centimetres tall can be an advantage, as can my wings."

"My name, though. I mean, really, what were my parents thinking? A fairy named Broomhilda?" She laughed. "It certainly makes me easy to remember. I just wish more humans believed in me. It would make my job so much easier."

My love for you will never end,

From then to now and always, I will speak to you with love,

From where I am to where you are,

Now and forever, across worlds and galaxies, across consciousness and throughout all our lives,

We are connected, through generations, through love,

Forever always...

So mote it be.

Forgiveness and Moving Forward

When we hold on to grief, regret and what ifs, we make ourselves ill; we allow dis ease to settle in.

Luna

Luna rubbed her knee. It didn't ache anymore, but she was so used to the pain from long ago that when the weather changed, she automatically rubbed her knee.

Reaching for a handful of spearmint leaves and a couple of raspberries from the pots on her verandah, she savoured the flavours, the sweetness of the healing herbs.

"I used to eat so much processed sugary foods, which only made the pain worse. Now when I crave chocolate or sugary treats, I have these, Yum!" Salem rubbed past his witch on his way to check out some movement in the strawberry patch.

"What have you found, my friend?" Luna followed her familiar. Salem rubbed his head on her arm as she found the last couple of strawberries.

"Good job Salem." She popped the strawberries into her apron for a snack later on.

"Ah, there it is." She pulled out the book she had popped into her apron weeks ago. Magic pockets in all her clothes meant that Luna was always finding things she had previously thought were lost. She flipped to today's date, so many years ago, and read the words she had once written.

Staying angry, sad, or frustrated only makes for more pain, anger, sadness and frustration. The trick to releasing these emotions lies in forgiveness and letting go. Not forgetting the wrongs done, but forgiveness for the transgressor and, more importantly, forgiving yourself.

STELLA

Stella also read those same words written in her journal.

"I can forgive myself. I have to, for healing to happen," Stella spoke to Puddles, her brand new kitten, snuggled up on her purple chenille blanket. Puddles was his name because only two days ago, Stella had been walking home across the park and found the soggy, wet, bedraggled tabby grey kitten caught up in a hessian sack.

"I don't want to stay angry with the father of my children. I don't want to forget or forgive either. But I need to forgive me for not being perfect. I was trying my best. I didn't understand about energy ripples and vibrations and empaths, or protecting ourselves or energy healing."

It was only on her journey through the hedge and the coven she visited in her dreams that Stella was learning about these exciting new energies. New energies that were actually as old as life itself. She flipped through *The Book of Spells* that she had found sitting on her kitchen bench two days ago, the same day she had found Puddles on her way home from work. Stella was grateful for whoever had left the book there for her. She was learning so much, reading through it.

"If I had known about these things, I would have made sure I taught my kids how to protect themselves, how to heal, just like I taught them right from wrong, reading, telling the time and how to bake cakes.

"Maybe I am magic, and that's why Andie and Emily are visiting more," she told her new friend.

"I can't continue to be sad because they aren't here all the time. Kids grow up and move away anyway. It is time to find other things to be happy and passionate about." Like her new kitten and trips through the hedge.

She smiled as Puddles buried his head next to hers on the bed. She loved her new friend, even though looking after him, settling him into his new home, meant travel through the hedge had to wait.

The childcare centre was happy for Stella to bring Puddles to work for the first couple of weeks. Teachable moments for the children. Luckily none of the children in her room were allergic to cat hair. In a world where everyone seemed allergic to nuts, eggs and even milk or bread, a room free of pet allergies was unheard of.

Stella's dreams had been full of images of Scotland, the coven and crowds. She had spent a restless two nights not quite asleep, feeling like she was remembering things, how to use crystals and herbs, casting spells and enchantments. The images and voices were muffled. No matter how hard she tried, she couldn't find her way back to the forest or the town where she had met Brigid.

"Patience," whispered the spirits as she snuggled up to Puddles.

"Soon, Puddles, I am going to try leaving you home alone. For a few hours at a time, then by next week, you should be okay here while I am at work, or somewhere else." She loved watching as he chased the fluffy orange ball she had found, her socks, her shoes and the blankets. She spent hours watching him play as she read the magical book.

Reading about being an empath and how to protect herself from the energy of others, it all made sense. There were spells and actions for protection, abundance, empaths, communication with spirits, travelling between worlds, and magical uses for herbs and crystals.

After years of not understanding the exhaustion or the emotional toll just going outside could cause, she was now starting to understand the panic attacks when she ventured to a shopping centre, or a sporting complex or concert with her children. She was learning how to conjure her invisible purple cloak before going out into the world.

Luna

Luna flipped through her original *Book of Spells* from so long ago. So many emotions, so many words and feelings and energies. As she flipped through the pages and found the first 'spell' she had cast so many years ago.

North and South, East and West,
Help me now, Do what is best,
Release the anger, regret and pain,
Guide me to myself again,
Find my passion find my love,
This I ask the heavens above...
So mote it be.

For both mother and crone, family was everything. Both mother and crone were also learning that the world and their lives were lived in cycles.

"Our identity and our sense of self change as we age and grow. Life is complex, whether we live alone or with others."

One of the most exciting truths both women had learnt along their magical journey was the art of manifestation.

LUNA

Luna thought back over her life, remembering all the times she had used manifestation to make her dreams come true.

"My little cottage and garden, I dreamt this place into being. I think I still have the pictures I drew of it, here somewhere."

Many years ago, she was drawn to the village only five kilometres away.

She had been hired as a cleaner for end-of-lease real estate cleaning. Five years into the job and she saw, in the real estate window, this little cottage up for sale at a reduced price, because it needed so much to be done to it to make it suitable for modern living.

As soon as she visited it, she knew it was hers. It was exactly as she had dreamt it. The picket fence, the walled garden, the vegetables and fruit trees. All neglected as if it had been abandoned a hundred years before.

Luna had spent the next ten years slowly building the garden back up, installing a second-hand water tank, a medicinal herb garden, and other nooks and crannies.

"Even you turned up because I dreamt you into being," she told Salem as he jumped up on the table where she was creating her next vision board. Cereal packet cardboard, pictures from junk mail and drawings and writing from her twenty-year-old textas. Her vision board this year focused on new plants she wanted to grow in her garden and a new design idea she had for her medicinal herb area.

"YOUR PREDECESSOR, MY last familiar, had passed on to the next stage of her journey, and I was lonely, missing my feline companion." She stroked his head as he nuzzled her hand.

She remembered sitting at this very table, drawing pictures of a tiny little black stray kitten. Within a week, she had found Salem hiding down the back of her garden under the mulberry bush.

Luna had learnt manifestation such a long time ago. She vaguely remembered her life before she learnt this superpower.

"I suspect that all the negative, drama and trauma in my life, and even in my past lives, had been a result of negative manifestation. The problem was I was worrying about and focusing on what I didn't want instead of what I wanted."

"I wonder Salem, did I make all the bad stuff happen? Surely people have free will and make their own choices."

Salem purred loudly from his position as he had wormed his way onto the crone's lap as she had been lost in her reverie.

Life had been tough for Luna until she had embraced her witchy-ness.

The black sheep of the family, she had never belonged. Ran away with a fella that was abusive and stayed for far too long because she didn't know that she didn't have to. Once she had enough and couldn't stand it anymore, she had left.

She had such a low opinion of herself that the next three relationships were just as abusive.

"It was only when I met Catherine and Tizzie that I started to understand that my opinions and ideas weren't all wrong, that my intuition and my thoughts were just as valid as everyone else." Under their guidance, her abilities and skills, her awareness and intuition had grown from strength to strength.

Manifesting

S tella

Stella was still learning about manifestation.

"Is it just as easy and simple as wishing something, for it to happen?" she wondered.

"My problem is, I have to really believe that I deserve it. I have to believe I can do it. I have to believe it is possible," she sighed as Harry the hermit crab scuttled around his terrarium. Harry was another new addition to Stella's animal family.

"You need a pet to talk to Mum, instead of that silly fairy. So Emily and I got you Harry." Andie surprised Stella the same day that Puddles had arrived. Andie had set Harry up in an empty terrarium that she found in the spare room while Stella dried Puddles. Mother and daughter had spent the afternoon settling the pets into their new home.

"My other problem might be focus and concentration," Stella mused as she found herself thinking back over that lovely afternoon.

"Maybe I am getting the hang of manifestation after all," she told Puddles, who was trying to keep up, wrapping himself around her feet to try to slow her down. She scooped him up and placed him in the playpen-like cage she placed in the living area. Complete with a cat climbing pole, a pillow, his kitty litter and toys.

She glanced at the clock. There was still an hour or so of daylight left.

"Puddles, I won't be long. You stay there, you have all your toys and stuff. I will see you soon."

This time when she opened her eyes, on the other side of the hedge, she was in a tunnel under a building. It was cold and dark, and she couldn't see very well.

"Keep calm," she whispered to herself as she felt the fear rising from the pit of her stomach.

Something told her to close her eyes. This made no sense to her logical mind, but her magical intuition insisted.

With her eyes closed, she felt her way along the wall of the tunnel. She heard men quarrelling. She made out the words sage and clove, but she couldn't hear exactly what they were saying.

"Should I turn around and go home? I do want to know what is happening, though," she thought, inching closer to the voices. She opened her eyes. To her right was a big open fireplace with pots hanging over them on a metal railing. There were benches along one side of the room. Floor-to-ceiling shelves similar to the shelves in the coven's workshop, laden with jars of all sorts of strange items. She guessed she was looking at a kitchen underneath a castle or maybe a stately home. Her eyes grew used to the candlelight coming from the kitchen. She noticed someone else in the shadows, also watching the scene in the kitchen. He was of a slight build, dressed in dark robes. He looked young, probably a similar age to her children.

As Stella turned back to watch what was happening in the kitchen, something didn't look right. From what she knew of history, women were the cooks and kitchen hands, not men. What she was watching in front of her was three men dressed in long hooded robes, huddled over the fire where a pot was bubbling and hissing. As she watched, from her position about ten metres away, the men poured the mixture from the pot into a set of three earthenware jars. Sealing each jar with lids made from cork, the tallest of the three men handed a jar to each of the others.

Stella glanced over to see if the other person was still in the shadows. He wasn't. He must have slipped away while she was focused on the happenings in the kitchen. By the time she looked back at the kitchen, it was empty.

"Where did they go?" she spoke aloud before she could stop herself.

"And how do I get out of here?" Looking back at the tunnel behind her, she gasped. The long tunnel was no longer there. Behind her, about five metres away, was a dead end. Bricks. No gaps that she could see. Feeling along the wall, with her eyes closed, did not reveal any hidden doors.

Moving swiftly and quietly into the kitchen, she realised it was more a workshop, similar to the coven's workshop, than a kitchen. She wrinkled her nose at the smell. Whatever they were making couldn't have been food.

"So what was it? A potion of some kind?" she whispered, although this time she was sure she was now alone in the room.

Remembering she had her phone in her pocket, she took photos of the jars and the pots on the shelves, the pans and pots on the fireplace, and the bits and pieces of herbs and other ingredients scattered on the workbench. She felt like it was important she had that information. Not sure why yet, but she was sure it would make sense later.

"Leave now," whispered her guides.

"How? Where?"

"Door," her guide's voice was sharper than normal. Stella looked around, trying not to panic, trying to find the door.

"Shadow." This time it was her intuition. She slipped into the darkest corner she saw. Pressed up against the wall, hiding from whatever danger was on its way. A hand reached out from behind, covering her mouth and pulled her through the wall!

Spinning around, Stella came face to face with Brigid from the tavern.

"I thought it was you," Brigid smiled, leading her to a bench seat at the back of the tavern. Seeing Stella's puzzled face, she continued. "I was working in the bar when I heard a voice calling me. I followed the voice, and there you were."

"Where was I?" Stella asked, "And how did I get here?"

"First, let me get you a drink, then an explanation." Brigid smiled.

Placing the two tankards on the table, Brigid slid into the seat beside her.

"The cellars of Dunnotter Castle. There are portals there. My best guess is that you entered a portal that led you there. Another portal transported us here."

Stella considered what she had heard.

"Do portals take us to different places? And can we choose where we go?"

"Yes, they do, and no, we can't always control where we will end up. It depends on the day, time of the year, and the magic used to manipulate the portal." Seeing the worried look on her friend's face, Brigid added, "We can get you home safely tonight as long as you leave before midnight."

Stella nodded, relieved.

"What was I watching in the castle tonight?"

"I'm not sure. Tell me what you saw."

"I saw three men huddled around a pot over a fire, making some kind of potion. They poured the mixture they had made into three clay jars. Then they disappeared. I didn't know about the portal then, but that must be where they went."

"Oh, and there was a younger man, not much more than a boy, watching them. He disappeared too. I realise now that he may have also moved through a portal." Stella finished breathlessly.

Brigid paused, taking a drink from her tankard. She checked the bar to make sure no one was waiting for a drink. The door opened, and a woman entered the tavern. Brigid beckoned for her to join them. Brigid introduced the two women.

"Stella. Maisie. Stella here stumbled upon Angus, Blair and Logan up to no good as usual. I think Archie was watching them."

"Do we need to do anything now?" Maisie asked.

"I'm not sure yet," Brigid placed her hand on Maisie's. "We need to ask Archie for more details. After we get Stella home safe, for now. If they saw her today, that changes things."

Turning to Stella, Brigid whispered, "This won't make sense now, but you need to go home, for now. Take this paper, and memorise the words when you get home, not now." Brigid passed a crumpled piece of paper to Stella under the table. Stella slipped the paper into her pocket, finding her phone.

She slid it out onto the table.

"I took photos," she told the others, "Pictures of what was in the room if that helps," she showed the women the photos she took under the castle. They huddled together so others wouldn't notice what they were looking at.

The other two women changed meaningful glances. Maisie slid Stella's phone back. "Thank you, that helps more than you know,"

Brigid continued, "Go home, memorise what you read. Go to work as normal and come back tomorrow night."

"We can explain more to you next time."

"One more thing. If you see Luna, Catherine and Tizzie tonight, tell them the storm is coming."

"Take this key. Keep it with you at all times." Maisie slid a key from her scarf and handed it to Stella. "For protection, and to focus your growing magic."

"Will the portal at the end of the alley take me home?" Stella whispered.

"Yes. If you hurry. Don't look back. We will meet here tomorrow evening," Brigid and Maisie each gave Stella a quick hug.

"Wait!" Brigid hurried over to the door with her, pulling a long robe off the rack behind the bar. She handed it to Stella. "It's yours. It will keep you hidden and enable you to move around unnoticed."

Stella smiled her thanks, not trusting herself to speak, concentrating on getting home safely. She donned the long brown robe, pulled the hood up over her head and exited the tavern.

Head down, she moved swiftly through the few people still out late. She felt eyes watching her but heeded her new friend's words and didn't look back.

Messages

S tella

The sky was just as dark back at the bottom of her garden. Relieved to be home, she hurried inside to check on her pets.

"I don't normally check if I have locked the doors and windows. Tonight feels like a night to make sure we are safe," she told Puddles as she tucked him into her robes. Harry was already tucked away in his house. She double-checked that all the doors and windows were locked as she turned out the lights. Hanging her new robes on her bedroom door, she extracted Puddles and hopped onto her bed. Her bedside clock told her it was just after midnight. Once Puddles was happily curled up in the blankets, Stella emptied her pockets. Her phone, the key Maisie gave her and the crumbled piece of paper from Brigid.

The photos from the castle were still on her phone. She poured over them, although they were a little blurry and grainy. "I'm so glad that these photos helped Brigid and Maisie."

She held the key in her hand. Made of dark grey metal, it was weighty for a key but small enough to fit on her necklace. Stella strung the key on her necklace with the tiny amethyst.

Finally opening the crumbled bit of paper, she read the words aloud.

"We are three, but we are one.

We make magic; we move between worlds. What was lost is now found.

We call on our clan—we remember.

Our worlds merge but heed—we harm no one, we listen to our guides, we see, we read, we hear and believe.

So mote it be."

Stella snuggled down, memorising the words. Clasping the key in one hand, snuggling Puddles in the other.

THE NEXT THING SHE knew, Stella was watching Luna, Catherine and Tizzie in the workshop. Noticing her, Tizzie beckoned for her to join them.

"The storm is coming," Stella blurted before even saying hello. "Brigid and Maisie wanted me to tell you that the storm is coming."

Feeling in her pocket for her phone, she passed it to Catherine and the others.

"This is a telephone. It takes photographs, pictures of things."

"I was in Dunnottar castle. I saw three men making a potion they poured into earthen jars. And a younger man watching them. I don't know where they went, but I think Brigid and Maisie were going to find out more." Stella paused, looking from one woman to the other for their reaction.

After a quick glance between the three witches, Tizzie responded, "That makes sense. We were waiting for that information." Seeing Stella's look, she continued. "When we first met you, we knew you. We also knew you didn't remember us, or maybe wouldn't remember us."

"We knew something was going to happen. If you found your way back to Brigid and Maisie, the portals must be open," Catherine added.

"It has also been stormy, more so than normal. This occurs every twenty seven years or so. It likely means that magic is growing in strength. Some magical beings get more powerful. Others discover they are magical. I suspect you are one of those who are only just now learning or remembering who you really are," Luna said.

"Time works differently over here," Tizzie confided. "We have all lived many different lives, in different realms, or worlds. Through portals, we can cross over between these worlds. We end up in different eras throughout history. Some realms are more like parallel worlds, where we live similar lives to the person we are now. Other realms have elves, fairies and other magical creatures living amongst humans." Tizzie held up a couple of bottles of different sizes, moving them around each other like planets moving around the sun.

"Magic has always existed. In some realms, it is driven underground. In some worlds, it is against the law. Some people practice quietly, helping heal people, like we do." Tizzie pointed to a row of jars filled with herbs, bark and seeds.

Catherine chimed in, "Others use magic for evil, to harm others. Angus, Blair and Logan don't normally cause trouble. They aren't malevolent. We do think they are planning something to help save magic and not to cause harm. We asked Archie to follow them. He hasn't returned."

"Here, in this realm, there are several groups; magical, non-magical, Scottish, English, good magic and bad magic, human and sprites, elves, fairies, and others." Tizzie paused and ducked out the door.

She returned less than a minute later.

"Archie is back. He followed them until they moved through different portals. He didn't follow any of them, so he doesn't know where they went." She plopped herself down on the long wooden seat near the workbench. "I asked him to go back and wait by one of the portals. He noticed a storm out over the castle, and another near the stones."

"Separate storms. I bet they are showing us where some of the portals are. Although it seems there are more portals opening each day," Catherine suggested. Her sisters nodded.

"You need to go back now." Luna turned to Stella. "There is much for us to do and not much time. We will gather ingredients for spells and enchantments and send messengers with messages to our friends in other realms. You will help Brigid and Maisie tomorrow night. You are their third. Our most effective spell work is in groups of three."

"Although sometimes there is one who is powerful enough alone," Tizzie added, "It will start to make sense, I promise."

"And thank you from all of us. Your help has been invaluable." Catherine smiled.

"How do I go back? A portal?" Stella asked.

"No, it's too dangerous with storms brewing." Catherine handed her a cup. "Drink this."

Stella drank down the warm thick tea, tasting aniseed and peppermint and a hint of clove.

The next thing she knew, she was back in her bedroom, and the sun was peeping through the curtains.

"I'm sure I am not making this up. I really am caught up in the middle of a magical mystery," she said as Puddles poked his head up from where he was snuggled under the lilac covers.

It was only five am and she didn't start work until six thirty. She was wide awake and excited. Tonight seemed like an eternity away.

She popped the piece of paper Brigid had passed her into one of the pockets of the robe hanging on her door.

"I didn't imagine this," she marvelled. Puddles sat up, watching her. "There is this robe, the key around my neck, and the note." She touched the key, safely attached to her necklace.

She pulled the piece of paper back out of the robe and took a photocopy. Then she also took a photo of it before tucking it back in the robes.

As she picked up the printed copy off the copier, she glanced at the calendar. It was already June. The fifth of June, to be exact. The year half over already. Her eyes were automatically drawn to June twenty-three. The date her world changed forever, so many years ago. When her father passed away. Many years later, on June twelve, her firstborn, Pedro arrived. A day of blessings and celebration.

Yule or Midwinter

June twenty-one sees the shortest and darkest of days, when there is more darkness than light. This time is called Yule or Midwinter. It is a turning point, though, as from this day on, the days get slightly longer again. There is still a long way to go before winter ends, but there is hope for the warmer days and a brighter future. Celebrations include creating yule logs, yule trees, and hanging mistletoe. Sounds a little like Christmas, another pagan celebration.

Luna

"A pagan celebration to celebrate God's son's birth," chortled Luna, enjoying the irony.

Forgive and forget,
Or Forgive but not forget,
We can still keep the lessons of the past when we forgive transgressions,
Remember life lessons,
But not let the past interfere or ruin our present and our future.
It is a balancing act,
And like the seasons and the years, it is a cycle.
We can always start again,

So mote it be.

LUNA

When Luna tried to remember her past, her distant past, her head hurt. People tended to pass through her life, visiting with her on her journey, for a time, before moving on. It took many years for the crone to be okay with losing people. That she would never be part of family celebrations. She had wept many tears until she had none left.

Then she remembered with gratitude the snippets from her past, when she had been blessed to be a part of special celebrations. Memories to be treasured forever.

Luna was grateful that she had found magic.

To celebrate Yule with gratitude, she lit a white candle in memory of all she had to be grateful for. She picked a few sprigs of the blue flowering rosemary in the giant blue pot just outside the door. Sitting with the rosemary and the candle, she chanted:

Memories good and memories bad,
Happy times and sad,
I release the pain, the anger and fear,
Bringing peace and happiness near.
So mote it be.

Luna believed the words she chanted. For years she had resisted happiness, not understanding that she was allowed to be happy. Now she realised that her plants and her pets made her happy, and she was okay with that. She looked fondly at Salem.

Salem stood to one side, knowing not to get in the way of the crone's spell work.

Stella

"Believing in myself." "That is the trickiest part of the whole thing." "How do I believe in myself when no one else ever has believed in my ability to do things?" "Am I being overly dramatic?"

Stella wasn't sure.

She had a couple of hours to fill in before her trip through the portal, and she wanted to see if she could perform some magic. She thought she would try some simple candle work.

She was determined to make the flame flicker and move in the direction she wanted it to.

"You have to believe," she told herself.

Another voice chimed in, "You have to believe."

She was used to hearing the voices, now. Her spirit guides, would often whisper clues and suggestions. Making the drive to work easier, helping her avoid annoying people, or when to go shopping to find the best bargains.

"Last night, I instinctively listened to the messages, in the tunnels, without question. I implicitly trusted my guides would keep me safe." Puddles was sitting at her feet, curled up on her slippers, purring and kneading with his tiny front paws.

"You have to believe." This time the voice was different, louder, "You have to believe in you."

Stella caught her breath as she heard the voice, even louder, at exactly the same time as she saw it.

No more than twenty centimetres tall, Stella blinked, watching the creature as it moved closer to her. It was wearing what looked like blue jeans and a purple shirt, with a purple sparkly cap and purple sneakers.

Stella blinked several times. The creature was human-like, and was moving closer.

"Okay, so now believe in me," the sarcasm was unmistakeable, even in someone so tiny, "and then believe in yourself." The creature laughed quietly at the look on Stella's face. "Allow me to introduce myself. My name is Lexie. I am a sprite, not an elf or a fairy, a pixie or even a goblin." She gave a funny little bow.

"I am here to help you because you are starting on your magical path."

Now that the initial surprise had passed, Stella had so many questions.

"So when I kept thinking there was something moving, just out of the corner of my eye, was that was you?"

Lexie nodded. "Me or one of the other magical folk who live around here."

"So do you teach me stuff from a book, how to be magical, or do magic spells?"

"That's not quite how it works," Lexie sat cross-legged right in front of Stella.

"You learn and discover things for yourself; we just hang around in case you need some help. In some cases, people can get carried away with their magic. Not everyone uses their magic for the right reasons. Sometimes there is a mess to clean up."

That made sense to Stella. She could imagine what would happen if people had access to magic and then decided they wanted to be rich and powerful. She shuddered at the thought.

"We don't think you are going to get into trouble," Lexie reassured Stella.

"Now, I want you to focus. Focus on believing in yourself. Focus on believing the magic is possible."

It was difficult to take her eyes off the sprite, but she did her best to follow Lexie's instructions. In less than five minutes, she could make the candle flame move in different directions. She turned to thank the sprite, but Lexie had disappeared.

"Thank you," Stella said, believing that Lexie could hear her.

Luna

Luna often saw sprites, elves, and fairies in her garden. After her initial surprise, she got used to them being around. She would talk to them, confide in them, consider them friends.

Trixie, the first sprite to have made herself known to Luna, had explained it like this.

"Not all humans are magical. All of the magical creatures you have read about in books are real; sprites, elves, goblins, fairies, pixies and others. We normally stay hidden from humans. Most humans don't understand magic.

"When humans start to believe in their magic, there is a sprite assigned to help them as they figure out what magic means for them.

"There is a frequency of magic that we tap into. Anytime you need us, we find you. Eventually, as you become more proficient, you won't need help. But we will always be nearby to assist if you need us."

LUNA'S FIRST SPELL had been for protection. Living in a flat in a city, there were always strangers around, and being an empath, the energies and emotions had driven her to distraction. Luna recited this chant three times.

Elements of the sun,
Elements of the day,
please come this way.

Powers of the Night and Day, I summon thee.
I call upon thee to protect me! So mote it be.

Picturing a golden ball of energy encasing herself and her home as she chanted the spell, she immediately felt a sense of calm. The protection spell kept Luna's energy safe and shielded from negative energy for months. Every six months or so, she grew stronger, and the protection spell, when she chanted it, afforded her years of protection each time.

Dreams Come True

S tella

Stella had her candle magic sorted and had started practicing with the golden ball of energy. She had been fascinated with the concept for a while and finally decided she was going to give it a go.

Her telephone rang right in the middle of her protection spell.

"Hello, Stella speaking.... Oh my goodness, really! Wow! Thank you so much!" Stella picked up the nearest pen and scribbled something down on the back of the envelope that contained a copy of Andie's school photographs.

"When? Goodness, that's awesome! Yes I will. Thank you so much!" She quickly made more notes in her messiest handwriting.

Stella put her phone down, feeling like pinching herself.

"I won! Puddles, I won!" She did a funny little dance, nearly tripping over her startled kitten.

"I don't normally bother to enter competitions," she told Puddles, still dancing around the living room, "But I have never travelled anywhere. I have only ever lived in a few places around here. When I saw the competition for an all-expenses paid trip to the other side of the world to witness the sun come up at Stonehenge on midsummer's morning, I just had to enter."

For the next two weeks, she had focused on the trip, manifesting how she would feel, what she would see and do when she was there. Putting all the manifesting skills she had learnt into action. She had actually believed it was possible.

"WOOHOO! WHOOP WHOOP!"

Puddles danced around her feet. Her excitement was contagious.

People who liked dogs thought cats were aloof and private. All Stella's cats had been familiar, friendly and cuddly. Even Spot, the stray cat that wandered into their lives when the kids were little, was friendly, if a little skittish. Puddles was one of the friendliest of them all. He followed Stella everywhere.

The summer solstice in the northern hemisphere was less than two weeks away. Deep in the middle of a Canberra winter, the idea of warmer weather was exciting, especially because she would be celebrating it at Stonehenge!

Stella thought back over every detail of the telephone call. She checked her notes to make sure she had all the details she needed.

Every single item of the trip was already paid for. The travel, accommodation, and all meals. She would be spending close to twenty-four hours in a very large aeroplane, with one stop over at Dubai. Once she reached London, she would get on a coach to a motel in a city near Stonehenge. Bright and early the next morning, the coach would take her and others out to Stonehenge. After a couple of hours, it was back on the coach for two days of sightseeing around London. Then it was back in the big aeroplane for the trip home.

To say Stella was excited was an understatement. June, the month with so much emotional baggage, now had an exciting new twist. For the first time ever, she was pleased that her children were with their father.

THE ALARM ON HER PHONE sounded.

"It's time!"

Stella popped Puddles into his cage, giving him an extra long cuddle.

"I'll make sure you are well looked after when I am overseas."

Remembering her robes, she grabbed them as she ran out the door.

Chanting the words from the paper in her pocket, Stella forced herself to calm down as she walked down the path and through the hedge.

Maisie was waiting for her as she arrived in the alley. The women hugged like old friends. Both glanced up as a clap of thunder banged overhead. They pulled their robes tightly around themselves and hurried to the tavern. Brigid was chasing out the last of her customers who didn't appreciate the earlier closing time and locked the door behind them.

"Rum on the bar. Drink up," Brigid hugged Stella as the thunder and lightning continued to rumble and flash outside. Stella drank her rum, marvelling at the totally different effect of drinking alcohol on this side of the portal. Here it sharpened and focused her. In her previous experience with alcohol, it dulled her senses. She wondered if the rum in the tavern was magical.

Brigid led both ladies to a table with a map. Stella recognised the town, the alley, the tavern, and also what she thought was the forest and the workshop where she had met Luna, Catherine and Tizzie. She counted ten stars on the map.

"Portals?" she asked, pointing to the stars.

"YES. WE ARE IN A UNIQUE position. Portals from here reach out around the world and through time. Years ago, humans started persecuting witches. Magical folk wanted to wipe out humans. Their spell backfired, and damage was felt throughout the realms. The portals were closed to keep everyone safe." Maisie continued, "Then, about two months ago, the portals started opening again. Magical folk began moving through realms."

"That in itself doesn't cause a problem. It's only when they try to use magic for the wrong reasons. Then something needs to be done," Brigid finished.

"The three men you saw last night are witches, like us. They were here the last time the portals had to be closed. They saw the damage that was happening when people from all realms could move around freely." Maisie continued, "We think that when the portals started opening again, they decided to take matters into their own hands. We aren't sure, but we think they are going to try to break all the portals."

"Last time the portals were disabled. Caretakers were nominated to keep everyone safe. Luna, Tizzie, Catherine, Logan, Angus and Blair.

"Every twenty-seven years, magic surges, causing the storms. Magic awakens in some people and strengthens in others. Portals open.

"Logan, Angus and Blair probably think they are doing the right thing." Maisie stopped to finish her drink. She held up her tankard for a refill.

"Can you talk to them?" asked Stella. She had also finished her drink but wasn't confident enough to hand it back to Brigid. She hadn't known these ladies long enough, and yet they felt like kindred spirits.

Brigid filled all three tankards, giving Stella a wink as if she could read her mind. "Yes I can, and yes we are, kindred spirits, that is."

Banging and yelling at the door made all three ladies jump.

"We know you are in there! Open up Brigid!" Loud male voices exploded inside the tavern as Brigid opened the door. Three men almost fell through the door, tumbling over each other in effort to stay on their feet. Brigid and Maisie snorted with laughter at the sight. Stella couldn't help smiling.

Two of the newcomers started chuckling as well. The tallest of the three, the only one who didn't see the funny side of the situation, frowned at his friends.

Brigid handed the men each a tankard as the mood in the tavern turned decidedly more serious. She scowled at each of them, forcing them to take a long drink before anyone spoke.

"We know that you are planning something. We think you might be trying to break the portals to stop magic spilling over like it did last time." Brigid paused and turned to Stella. "If you haven't already guessed, this ragamuffin bunch are Logan, Angus and Blair."

Logan, the tallest of the three men, nodded at Stella.

"We know who you are. The portals started opening when you discovered magic. You are the key, but we don't know why. With the portals open, all kinds of magical creatures are travelling between the worlds." Logan turned back to face Brigid. "You are right. We did plan to break the portals, to stop magic being used for the wrong reasons, to keep everyone safe."

"WE KNOW YOU CAN TRAVEL here through your dreams, so you will still be able to visit after the portals are broken." Blair continued, directing his comments at Stella. He was the shortest of the three and had long blonde hair tied back into a ponytail. Logan's hair was much darker and shorter.

"We met with the elves yesterday, and Angus here met with the goblins. Both groups asked us to reconsider breaking the portals. They made a good case for keeping the portals undamaged. We might need to travel through them in the future. Other realms have also sent word that they don't want the portals broken. We don't want to ruin magic. We just want to keep everyone safe. We are happy to work on options so that all the groups are happy." Blair held up his tankard with a cheeky smile. "Any chance of a refill?"

"We still need a way to stop magic being collected for evil," Logan insisted, holding his tankard up as well.

Maisie stood up, collecting the tankards for Brigid to refill them. She passed the tray over to the bar. "Brigid and I heard from Luna today. She suggested we all work together to close the portals. Not break them, but to place an enchantment on them, with a secret charm on them so they only open under certain conditions."

"That might work," Logan conceded. "We do have a week or so before we have to decide."

Stella stood up. "I have a question."

Brigid nodded.

"Why can I open the portal, and why can I travel in my sleep? And why now?"

The Explanation

Brigid motioned for Stella to sit down next to her.

"Centuries ago, magic could be found throughout Scotland. There were goblins, elves, sprites, fairies, even dragons. Most families had at least one magical person. A mage, wizard, or witch; who looked after the families, protecting them from evil. Evil was also far more common, magical evil, not just regular bullies," she said.

"Magical folk, tended to live for centuries," Logan added. "So the same magician or witch would have protected several generations of the same family."

"About a hundred years ago, a group of witches decided to rid the land of all non-magical folk," Blair took over the story. "Their plan backfired, and instead of wiping out all humans, we thought they had, in fact, destroyed magic."

Maisie piped up, "Humans suffered too. There were droughts, famines and wars. Without the wisdom of the magic, people fought each other. They tricked each other and robbed and ruled badly. It was a dark time for our world. A few magicians and witches survived. They hid in other realms, with the remaining fairies, elves, sprites and goblins. They shared their knowledge with those who were chosen to keep magic alive. You have met Luna, Catherine and Tizzie."

Stella nodded.

Brigid continued, "Luna, Catherine and Tizzie mentored Logan, Angus and Blair. Maisie and I hung around with them and learnt as well. Magic had always been a part of our lives, but we needed training and focus. We have been practising magic, spells and rituals. Since the portals are closed, there have been no specific dangers or evil to challenge us. We do keep an eye out to make sure non-magical people are safe. The other magical folk look after each other. It has all worked well."

"Maisie and I have known for some time that we would meet you. Your ancestors are from one of the magical families of Scotland from long ago. You had to have your children, and they had to grow and leave home before your magic could awaken before you could find us.

"When Luna, and the others closed the portals, Luna lost her children. They disappeared, or they were taken away. To this day, no one is sure what happened. No one could ever work out why, or where they went, even with magic. So it was decided that we had to wait for you. So your children would be safe."

Stella considered everything she had just been told. Strangely it all made sense. Before she could formulate any words, Logan spoke up.

"The magic surges, the storms, and the portals opening are linked to your magic awakening. We have heard about this happening before, many years ago. We are monitoring what is happening to ensure no evil takes advantage of the increase in magic. The balance between good and evil mustn't be compromised."

"We have heard from the folk in other realms about a group of magicians who are collecting magic from all the realms," Angus added. "We are worried they might be trying to complete what was started many years ago. To get rid of all non-magical beings."

"So how can I help?" Stella asked, "I don't know much about magic yet, but if I am here, I must be able to help somehow."

"If we are to succeed, we must close the portal from your side. It is not going to be easy," Logan continued, "We have to use ancient magic. Also, the portals have to be closed during the summer solstice."

Stella gasped, "Oh my goodness!" She jumped up, knocking over the tankards in her excitement.

"Lucky they were empty," Blair hinted to Brigid. "I would hate to have wasted any ale," he grinned.

"So what's up?" Maisie turned to Stella.

"Before I came here tonight, I won a competition to visit Stonehenge on the morning of the summer solstice. That can't be a coincidence, can it?" Stella started pacing. She was so excited and focused that her magical energy was sending electric sparks out, like tiny firecrackers. "You know what Stonehenge is, don't you?"

Everyone in the room burst into laughter. "Yes!" they chorused in unison.

Blair ducked one of the sparks, and Angus deflected one with his tankard.

Logan steered Stella back to her seat at the table, placing her hands on her tankard. Brigid had refilled all the tankards while Stella was speaking. Logan eyed the tankard in front of Stella and looked at Brigid, "The last thing this girl needs is more coffee!"

Everyone laughed.

Maisie and Brigid reached over, taking Stella's hands. Brigid smiled before saying, "Closing the portals from your side, at Stonehenge, on the summer solstice is just perfect! That's about two weeks away, less, is that right? I am sure the time is the same for us, even though the seasons are different."

"Yes, it is June where I live. I am looking forward to the warmth of the summer solstice. What do you need me to do?"

Brigid took a long drink of her tankard. Although she had filled the tankards not long ago, most of the group had already drained theirs.

"We have less than two weeks. We need to consult with Luna, Catherine and Tizzie. Maisie and I can do that," Maisie nodded as Brigid continued. "Angus, Logan, Blair, can each of you visit your main contacts in the other realms and let them know what we are planning, but wait until after we confirm with Luna and the others. We all meet back here at the same time tomorrow night to confirm the next steps.

"Stella, you need to practice your magic. Use the book that was gifted to you. It has all the knowledge you need to start." Stella nodded, remembering the *Books of Spells* that arrived on her bench a few weeks ago.

"The most important ingredient in any spell is you and your belief. That seriously is the most important factor Stella," Brigid's tone was that of the strictest teacher.

Stella nodded. "Yes. I am learning that. I was practicing today before I came here."

"Good girl. Do you think you can complete all the work in that book in a week, as well as getting ready for the trip and visiting us?" Maisie asked, a look of sisterly concern on her face. The boys all leaned forward, watching her, waiting for her answer and any indication that she wasn't up to the task.

Stella sat back, breathing slowly to calm her nervous energy. She considered the question and everything she was being asked to do. Her mind went back through all the times she doubted herself. She remembered how she had felt in the afternoon when she had believed in herself and her ability. It was like something clicked, and she finally knew who she was. Everything she had gone through had brought her to this place, now. She was more than just a daughter, or a mother or a teacher or a friend. She was a witch with an ancient power that couldn't be explained by logic. The reasons didn't have to be clear for her to believe. She stood up, drained her tankard, then answered the question.

"Yes. I can get all that done. I do believe in myself. I believe I can do this. I can learn everything I need to, get ready for the trip, work and visit here as often as I need to."

She felt everyone's eyes on her, scrutinising her face, her stance for any sign of weakness or fear. She held their gaze, each of them, one by one.

"Well golly, I do believe she can do this!" Logan stood up and punched the air. "We can do this! Woohoo!"

"Woohoo!" yelled all three boys, punching the air. Maisie and Brigid raised their tankards. The energy in the room was electric.

"One more drink each, then it's early to bed. Tomorrow is a big day for all of us," Brigid said, pouring them all one last tankard full of rum, adding a large coffee in Stella's. Sipping her drink, Stella looked around at the group in front of her. She smiled, feeling she belonged in this little tavern on the other side of the world.

Cycles and Seasons

W *e can reinvent ourselves every day, every week, every month. There is a season for everything.*

Luna

The cycle of life, the seasons, the years and their celebrations follow a pattern that stays the same. This brought comfort to Luna. The certainty that day will follow night and that spring follows after even the longest and coldest of winters.

Her altar sat along the west wall of her cottage. The sun shone on the altar first thing in the morning, and the moon shone through to the altar in the evening. Luna changed the altar depending on her spell work or the time of the year.

The small dish of soil, representing the earth element, reminded Luna to stay grounded and centred. The feather that Maude had gifted Luna years ago represented air and mental clarity. Emotions and water were symbolised by the little glass chalice, and a small white candle for the fire of creation. The element of spirit was created through movement as she performed rituals.

The sound of Maude screeching startled Luna. The magpie was normally the most softly spoken bird, crooning and warbling to Luna and the other birds. The commotion was so unusual that Luna dashed out to see what was happening.

"Salem stay back until I know it's safe!" Salem didn't want to stay where he was, but something in Luna's voice made him curl back up on the bed where he had been snoozing.

"Maude, what the devil?" Luna reached the door to see a couple of creatures shaking leaves at Maude, trying to dissuade her from getting any closer.

"Maude! Stop! They are friends and are hardly dangerous. They are less than half your size." Luna admonished her, tossing a handful of Maude's seed away from where the creatures were seeking shelter.

"I'm so sorry," Luna scooped down and picked up her friends.

"Thanks Luna!" The smaller of the sprites rasped. His voice reminded her of sandpaper. "I'm Bert, this is Gert," he gestured to the sprite beside him.

"Nice to meet you both. What brings you here? I imagine you didn't just happen to call past on your way somewhere."

"True, true," Bert responded. "We have a message from Catherine. She needs you. She knows you are comfortable here, but there is work to be done." Luna sat down on her chair, placing Bert and Gert gently on the arm of it.

"Magic is surging." Gert piped up. Her voice was nearly as gruff as her brothers. "Portals are opening across the realms. Magicians are taking magic from the realms. We need you to help keep everyone safe. We will look after your family and your cottage." Luna watched as Bert and Gert grew until they were the size of six-year-olds.

The old Luna, the one who didn't hesitate when there was work to be done, replied, "Of course. Thank you for staying here with Maude and Salem." At the sound of their names, Maude flew down and sat on her perch, and Salem wandered out and sat in front of his babysitters.

"You be good for Bert and Gert," Luna spoke to her each in turn. "If you misbehave, I will know."

Turning to Bert, she asked, 'I closed the portal in the house last week, how do I get back?'

Gert pointed towards the back of the cottage.

"You will see it, down the back, at the biggest tree. We will keep Maude and Salem occupied. Go now. Catherine has everything you need."

Luna was already lacing up her old, worn black boots that she kept on the porch. Giving Salem a quick pat and a wave to Maude, Gert and Bert, Luna walked briskly down the side of her cottage to the tree. She saw the portal straight away.

"I hope Catherine kept my spare robes." Looking down at her clothes, she was grateful that she had fallen asleep in her leggings and purple shirt rather than her purple flannel pyjamas. Feeling into her pocket, she found her key and rose quartz necklace. She popped it over her head and tucked it into the collar of her shirt.

Luna felt the familiar surge of magic energy as she stepped through the portal.

Catherine met her on the other side, in the tavern where they had spent so many years together. Tizzie, handed Luna her robes as Catherine passed her a mug of coffee. Putting both on the closest table, Luna embraced her old friends. All time and distance melted away as the three crones were together again.

Stella

Stella also had an altar of sorts, having cleared a shelf in her study. On the shelf sat a picture of her four children, a candle, a clear quartz, an amethyst and a rose quartz. She loved that photo of the children, before the rift. Her gaze shifted to the drawings she had hung beside the bookshelf. She would never tire of looking at these drawings. Created at a time when the world was less complicated.

Stella now understood that the time for grief and regret was over. Seasons change, and people change and grow. Like the phases of the moon, so it was with moods and emotions.

Energised by the events of the last twenty-four hours, Stella grabbed her coffee and her laptop and started planning. She had twelve days until she hopped on that aeroplane.

"Luckily I have my passport already. I can tick that off my list," she told Puddles, who sensing something was up, was sitting on the stool next to her.

"I'm going to take at least two weeks annual leave, maybe longer. A week to give me time to get everything done for the trip. Then the week of the trip." Stella remembered the conversation just last week with her supervisor, who mentioned that Stella had far too much leave accrued and that she needed to work out when she wanted to take some.

"Clothes aren't a big deal. I will just pack a couple of days before." Stella grabbed the information she printed from the email, providing all the details of the trip. There was a list of what items she could take on the flight, as well as what things weren't allowed. The list included other items that she needed to know on her first trip overseas. She tucked the paperwork into a clear plastic folder she took from the bookshelf. Carrying it to the spare room, she placed it on the bed with her passport and the luggage she planned to take.

"Now for the important part, the spell work." Stella picked up the *Book of Spells,* turning to the page with the protection spell.

"I did it!" Stella whooped five minutes later as the golden ball of energy she had conjured bounced around the room before disappearing into each of the four corners.

The next page was a detailed description of casting a circle. As Stella needed to buy some salt and some more candles before she could complete that one. She turned the page and found the incantation for an invisibility cloak.

"Now this sounds like fun. I can see why some people get carried away when they use magic. How easy would it be to use this spell to spy on people or steal or cause a huge amount of grief," Stella mused.

"I wouldn't do any of those things," she added hastily as Lexie appeared on the shelf next to her altar.

"I know you wouldn't," Lexie sat crossed-legged on the clear quartz tumble stone. "I am just watching. I am here if you need some help. This isn't the easiest of spells. Learning by yourself can be tricky sometimes. You don't seem to be having any issues, though." She watched as Stella created her cloak of invisibility. Magic sparks crackled and hissed as she moved her hands, muttering the magic words.

Stella practiced for an hour until she was able to bring her cloak to her with a click of her fingers. Lexie clapped. "Well done!"

The alarm on her phone reminded her of the time.

"Can I show you something tricky?" Lexie asked, hopping down off the shelf.

"Sure."

"Normally you have to train for months, but watching how easily you created your invisibility cloak, I think you are ready. May I?" Stella nodded as Lexie motioned to the book. Flipping forward five pages to the page titled Creating a Portal, Lexie pointed to the words.

"If you say these words and use the same magic and energy you used to create your cloak, clicking your fingers, you should be able to create a portal here, in this room. It might take you a few attempts, but I think you can do it. Just make sure you are thinking of where you want to end up. Concentrate on the spot, time and place.

"If you lose focus or concentration, you could end up somewhere you don't want to be. If that does happen, though, just say the words again and focus on coming home," she added.

Stella nodded, read the words, stepped into the middle of the room and pictured the middle of the tavern where she first met Brigid. She took a deep breath and waved her right arm in the same movement she had used to conjure her cloak. Speaking the words Lexie had pointed to, she clicked her fingers.

She had barely finished muttering the words when she landed in Brigid's tavern right in the middle of an animated argument.

"Stella!" Maisie exclaimed.

Brigid put her hand out to steady Stella as she swayed, the sheer momentum of the magic and energy overwhelming not only her but the others in the room as well.

The Magic Council

"The lady knows how to make an entrance!" Blair clapped. The others joined him in applauding the newest witch in the room.

"How many attempts?" Angus asked.

"First time," Stella blushed.

"Really? Well done!" Catherine came over and gave her a big hug.

Tizzie handed her a tankard. "Brigid said coffee, not rum. Luna is the same. Crazy ladies, why ruin good rum with coffee." She smiled.

"Thanks!" Stella realised she was thirsty after her afternoon's magic work. "So what did I interrupt? It sounded like an argument." She looked around at her friends.

"Actually, I have another question first. If I can create a portal and end up here, what is the point of closing the portals? Won't everyone just open their own portals?"

It was the quietest the tavern had been since Stella had started visiting. The others looked at each other. Stella looked around at her friends, wondering what she had said. Logan and Blair were looking at the floor. Angus shuffled his feet. Finally, Luna spoke up.

"To answer your second question first, not everyone can open a portal as easily as you can. I can't, and I have been practicing for many years." The crone touched the key on the cord around her neck. "I did open a portal once. But I think that was more good luck rather than my skills or abilities."

"IF WE, YOU, CLOSE THE portals on the summer solstice, it will make it harder for anyone to open one, at least for twenty years. Because you can open portals, it is highly likely that you will be able to close them, using the magic of the Stones to keep them closed for as long as possible. We are guessing this based on our shared histories through the realms. Each time the magic comes back stronger. This isn't guaranteed to work, but it is one of the best ideas we have," Blair said.

"The answer to your first question is that we were arguing about the best options," Catherine interjected. "We all agree we need to close the portals. Logan, Blair and Tizzie think we should do more than just close the portals. They want to stop all travel between worlds, to stop anyone stockpiling magic. The rest of us aren't too sure. We don't want to limit everyone's movements."

"To be honest, we aren't even sure what more we could do," Brigid added.

Stella looked around the room. Suddenly it all made sense to her. She couldn't believe she hadn't thought of this before.

"I have an idea."

Everyone crowded around her, leaning forward across the table.

Stella looked at each of her new friends.

"We each have specific magic skills. I think each of you knows people and magical creatures in other realms." Stella looked up as Brigid and Maisie nodded in agreement. "There are so many different types of folk, humans, magicians, elves, sprite, fairies."

"Dragons, ogres, dwarves, and others," Blair added.

Stella continued.

"We all have our own magic, energies and vibrations. So then every being who has magic would have a unique energetic vibration, is that right?" she looked around as they again all nodded in agreement.

"So do we have a magic council? A group of folks representing each realm?"

"Because if we don't, can we set one up in a week? If we had folk in each realm cast a circle to balance the magic storm in their realm at the same time as I close the portals, I think that would add the extra layer of security. Having each group involved might discourage others from trying to cause trouble."

Silence.

"That is crazy," Logan muttered, shaking his head. "It is so crazy that it just might work."

"We don't have a council, but I remember stories of a group like that many years ago when magic was as common as technology is now. Well, in the world you are in," Luna spoke up. "The stories we were told was that the council kept magic in balance. As long as the council worked effectively together, there was balance."

"Would it work now?" Blair asked.

"Could we get it organised in a week?" Tizzie wondered, "I know we have contacts in each of the worlds. Logan, could we get to each group in time?"

"IF WE LOOK AT THIS another way," Catherine posed, "Instead of contacts from each world or realm, could we find a rep from each group?"

"How many realms are there?" Stella asked.

"The thing is, no one knows. It seems to change," Angus said, moving the tankards around on the table. "It is like we can drop in and out of different ages, like you landing here about three hundred years before you were born." He moved the tankards into another order. "The portals open randomly."

Luna thought about Stella's proposal. "We can send out the message for someone from each group to meet with us. Logan, you, Blair and Angus know the right contacts. Let them know this is important. We have to meet and make some decisions. We can meet at the fairy glen."

Brigid stood up, moving swiftly behind the bar and returning with several decanters. "I think we all deserve a drink. We have a plan that I think will work. Does everyone agree?"

The others nodded.

"Three night's time. At the fairy glen." Luna stood up and held her tankard high in salute to everyone around the table.

Putting her arm around Stella, Maisie suggested, "You come here first, and we will go together. It can be tricky to move through the portal to somewhere you haven't been before." Stella nodded.

Luna

The crone was surprised at how easily she settled back into the coven with Catherine and Tizzie. Magic pulsed through her veins, stronger than before.

Broomhilda

Broomhilda smiled. She had been impressed by the conversation she had overheard from her hiding spot under the bar at Brigid's.

The Fairy Glen

Stella

Two nights later, the gathering at the fairy glen was buzzing with magic. Sparks flew around, and fairy wands glowed around the glen. Stella looked around at the group. There were fairies, elves, sprites, goblins, and other creatures she couldn't name. She was reminded of the story of Noah's ark. Except in this case, there were two, three or four of each group. She stood silently, watching and listening as Logan started the meeting.

"Okay everyone, listen up," Logan said as he stood up on one of the stones on the outside of one of the fairy circles. "You know why we are here. Magic is surging, and we need to ensure everyone's safety. We think we have a way as long as we work together." He paused. "We are here because we agree that we need to do something. As representatives for our groups, we can make sure that magic remains available for everyone and not collected and used to evil or destroyed."

"But what if it doesn't work?" Piped up one fairy from the front of the crowd.

"What if it is dangerous, and we get hurt, or worse?" the deeper voice of an elf from the back of the group asked. The other elves around him nodded in agreement.

"What if we destroy magic? Or it destroys us?" Another fairy at the front asked nervously.

"Why do we think she can do anything? Where did she come from?" A few voices throughout the crowd started muttering, restless, worried and anxious.

The group turned angry, fuelled by fear and uncertainty. Yelling out their concerns and pointing at Stella.

Stella stood up on the nearest stone so she was standing taller, with an air of authority. Hoping she sounded more confident than she felt, she addressed the group.

"I understand your concerns and your fears. You are right. It mightn't work. We might fail. But we have to do something. If we don't, we fail our people, evil wins, magic either gets out of control or is destroyed, or both." She turned, making sure she caught the eye of each creature in the crowd that was gathered in the glen.

"I am only new to magic. I have failed before in my life. But now I have been gifted with this magic, and fate has connected me with this group. Together you are the most powerful group in the realm. I only failed before because I didn't believe in myself or my abilities. Now I do believe in me and in each of you. I know I can do this. I know each of you can do this. Otherwise, we wouldn't be here."

As Stella held the gaze of the group, she noticed the sky. The muted dusk colours, normally a greyish yellow, were a vibrant purply pink. The colour seemed to shimmer and glow. Stella assumed she was looking at the phenomenon known as the northern lights. Some of the gathering gasped, noticing the sky changing too.

"Look over there!" One of the elves pointed, Stella turned to see the trees swaying as if dancing.

The energy and magic in the air was so strong Stella could almost see it. "Did I do that?" she wondered to herself.

Maisie waved her arms, attracting the attention of the crowd. "If you doubted Stella before, here is the proof. As she was speaking, the very world around us woke up. The vibrations and the magic in everything around us connected with Stella and also with each of us. I can feel it. I know you can too."

Luna moved to stand next to Stella. "Can we have a show of hands? Who agrees with what we are proposing to do?"

Luna, Stella and the others held their breath, waiting to see what the group gathered in the fairy glen would decide. One by one, most of the fairies, the elves, the sprites and the others raised their hands. A few members of the group looked at each other, whispering to their neighbours. Neither Stella nor Luna could hear what was being said.

Logan spoke up, "I have known most of you all my life. I wouldn't ask you to agree to anything if I didn't believe it would work. I wouldn't suggest a solution that would harm anyone."

Blair and Angus joined Logan.

"We believe this is the best option," Blair told the group.

"We believe Stella found us for this reason," Angus added. "We are asking you to believe us, to trust us."

One of the elves in the group turned to the others. "They are right. We can't just do nothing. We know these guys. They wouldn't steer us in the wrong direction. I say we back them."

"So, do we have a yes?" Logan asked the assembled group.

As Stella and the others watched, the rest of the group nodded their agreement.

"Blair, Angus and I will be in contact over the next day with the details. We have just over a week to put our plan together." The crowd started to disperse as Logan finished speaking. The moon shone down on the nine left behind at the fairy glen.

"THAT WENT WELL," CATHERINE stated. The others nodded in agreement.

"It's time for sleep," Tizzie stated the obvious, as the darkness was well and truly descending in the fairy glen. "Luna, Catherine and I will work out the details of the spell to cast. Logan, Blair and Angus, we will get the details to you as quickly as we can, so you can go and share it with those that were here. They will have their own version of magic to use for this as well."

"We will make sure Stella is ready," Brigid said.

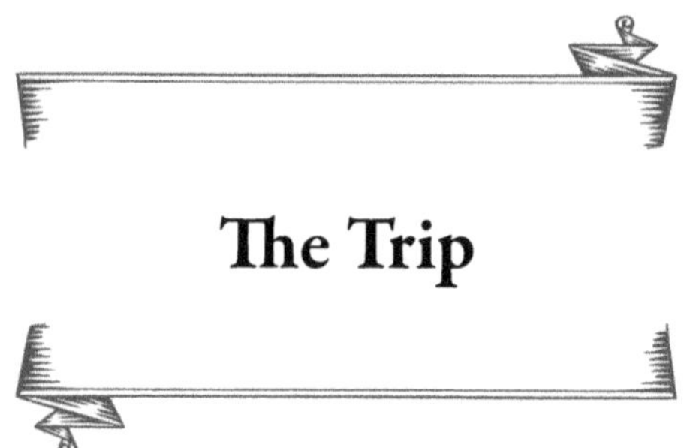

The Trip

Stella visited Brigid and Maisie only once more before her trip.

"There isn't much we can share with you in such a short time that you don't already know or have learnt from the book we left you," Brigid said as she handed a tankard to Stella. She then sat next to Maisie at their table at the back of the tavern.

"This is from Luna. It has the words for the incantation. It has a drawing of the stones you need to stand by. Also, the pouch contains the herbs you will need." Brigid gave Stella a small material bag no big than the size of her palm.

"We have made you a bracelet infused with magic. It will protect you and focus your intentions when you need it. It will make it easier for you to do your magic unseen by others," Maisie said as she tied a leather woven strap around Stella's wrist.

"The leather is hundreds of years old, and we wove some amethyst and rose quartz into it." Brigid pointed out the finest of chips in amongst the brown and tan straps.

"Oh, it's beautiful!" Stella stood up and hugged her friends.

"That's it then," Maisie said. "We know you can do this. You have the power, and you have been chosen. Remember what we taught you, and what you have learnt."

Brigid smiled at Stella, "I couldn't have said that any better. Have fun on the trip. Don't take it all too seriously. Come back and tell us all about everything."

"OKAY PUDDLES, KIM NEXT door will look after you and Harry while I am away." She scribbled a note for her neighbour, who had kindly offered to mind her pets.

She placed her suitcase across the door to the spare room so she could practise magic without harming Puddles. "I don't want you to end up in my invisibility cloak. Plus, I need to focus. Focus is the key." Stella cast her circle, focusing on the chant and the candles she had placed at north, south, east and west. Soon she had the golden ball of energy balanced above her hands.

Later as she finished packing for her trip, she realised she wouldn't be able to take her pouch of herbs with her. "I'll have to find them once I land. That might be a bit tricky, but I am sure I will figure it out." She gave Puddles a big hug as she locked her door, tucking her key and the note into the hanging plant as she had arranged with Kim.

"This is so exciting," Stella thought as she stepped into the cab that was to take her to the airport.

"I can actually feel the magic all around me." Stella remembered that Luna had taught her how to sit straight and concentrate on her breathing to calm the electrical energy that bounced around her when she was excited.

"It makes sense now." She remembered how electrical stuff would randomly turn on or off when she was really sad, or angry, like when the rift happened and she lost her kids. She quickly caught her thoughts and focused instead on the present. The prize included all taxi fares, all meals, accommodation and even spending money!

Stella watched out the window as the taxi weaved through suburbia. "I will never doubt the power of manifesting, or magic again. I know that I can create the future of my dreams." The taxi driver was singing to himself, paying no attention to his passenger in the backseat. Stella continued talking to herself, her excitement bubbling over like one of those volcanoes made from cola and lollies. "I ordered my passport, to convince myself I could travel overseas anytime I wanted to. How exciting!" Stella, held her hands in front of her, calming her breathing and her energy.

"I know I am a little early. I wanted to be sure I was here on time. I have never travelled overseas before." She thanked the cab driver, who pointed out that she was three hours early for her flight. Thankful she had applied for her passport a year ago, as part of her determination to look forward to new adventures. Something always seemed to get in the way and distract her. Until now.

Squinting at the signs, Stella followed the directions to the luggage drop and customs. With no more travel restrictions, the airport was bustling with people, all hurrying about, serious frowns on their faces as they moved through the various stages of arrival or departure.

"This is so much easier than I thought it would be," she thought to herself as she moved through customs without any problems.

Everyone was so nice and friendly. She had been unsure of the protocol with luggage. The customer service operator had been so helpful and explained it all so that Stella was able to breeze through without a problem.

"When we print out your ticket, there is a sticker for your luggage here. The big half folds across the handle of your suitcase, so we know which plane to send your luggage to. The small section goes on the back of your ticket, so we can locate your bag if it does get lost." Your carry on luggage is just the perfect size. You can place it in the overhead locker or under the seat in front of you if you prefer."

"Thank you so much!" Stella was appreciative of the extra information. She couldn't decide if the airline steward knew she was a first-time flier or if she was always this friendly.

"No problem! The departure gates are through there after you go through the security area. You have a couple of hours to wait for your flight. There should be some seats near the cafes and duty-free area. There are lots of different options for food or drink while you wait."

Stella thanked her again, almost skipping over to security.

Because Stella had never flown before and didn't know what to expect, she had read up on the rules. She didn't have any liquids in her carry-on luggage. She wasn't wearing any jewellery or anything that would set off the scans. She simply put her laptop in a separate tray as she passed through with everyone else. The whole experience had been a lot easier than she thought.

"There are so many great books here. I would love to read some of these," Stella had decided to fill in time by browsing through the shops as she waited for her flight.

Twenty-four hours in two planes, with a stopover at Dubai.

"I think I could get used to this," Stella thought.

All food and drink were free on the aeroplane. Each main meal included several food groups, and there were special diet plates available too. As much coffee, wine, juice or water as she asked for. The seats were fairly comfortable, and everyone was given a pillow and a blanket to sleep. Not that she slept at all. On the monitor on the back of the seat in front of her, she could watch movies, listen to the radio and play at least twenty different puzzle games. She could watch the flight on an interactive map or turn on the little light and read.

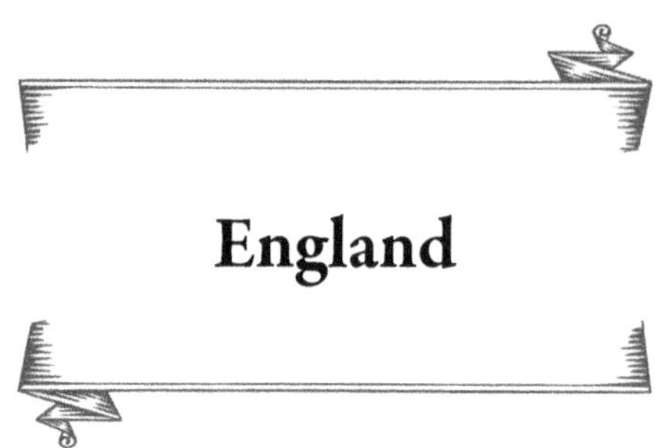

England

Stella

Twenty-three hours after leaving Australia, Stella was in England.

Stella followed everyone else through customs to the luggage pick-up. She overheard a couple talking about catching the shuttle to the south terminal to pick up a coach. She decided to follow them to make sure she found the right place.

Stella had no idea what the time was at home after almost twenty-four hours in the air. It was three o'clock in the afternoon in the United Kingdom when she hopped onto the coach. Two hours later, they arrived at the hotel in Salisbury. Stella followed two women who had talked nonstop the whole way from Gatwick and lined up at reception.

"Hi My name is Chantal. Welcome to The Stones Hotel." The receptionist smiled at Stella.

"I'm Stella. I won a competition to come over to England and visit Stonehenge."

"It is so lovely to meet you!" Chantal beamed, "How long have you been in the UK?"

Stella looked at the clock behind Chantel. "About three and a half hours."

"How exciting! Your room is down the hall, number one hundred and three. The restaurant opens at six pm. In the morning, if you are ready early enough, we can get you a cuppa and a snack for the trip to Stonehenge. It will be an early start, after such a long trip too." Chantel handed Stella her room key and a certificate for a meal in the restaurant.

"Thanks so much! I will be awake early enough. At this point, I am so excited I don't think I will sleep again until I am home. There is just so much to see. It is my first time overseas,."

"Aww honey that's awesome! Congratulations, and I hope you enjoy your trip."

STELLA COULDN'T BELIEVE how great her room was.

"This must be a king-size bed. It's so much bigger than my double bed." Stella sat and bounced on the bed. The paint on the walls was a deep teal blue. The curtains were a plush velvety brown that blended well with the walls. The floorboards were cedar wood.

Opening the door to the bathroom, she was a little worried there might have been a bath instead of a shower. She knew that English people generally preferred baths to showers. She needn't have worried.

As she splashed cold water on her face to freshen up, Stella realised she had forgotten to collect the herbs she needed for the next day.

"I didn't see any shops nearby." Stella blamed herself for not having slept for over twenty-four hours. "How could I have forgotten something so important?" She flopped down on the bed.

"Now what am I going to do?" Her head hit a bump on the pillow. She examined the pillow more closely. Tucked in the side was a pouch, no bigger than the palm of her hand.

Her heart pounding loudly in her chest, she opened the pouch. Inside, she found a mix of herbs, like a potpourri, and a note with the words: *For Stonehenge.*

"Thank you!" she said aloud to whichever magical folk had visited to make sure she had the right mix of herbs for closing the portal.

She tucked the pouch safely into her purse, which was tucked into the lining of her long purple cardigan. Stella was thankful that summertime in the United Kingdom was mild.

"I'd never wear my cardigan in summer at home."

She felt the piece of paper with the spell and the map folded safely in her purse. Her necklace held the key, the amethyst and a tiny locket with a photo of her kids.

She took the birthday candle and mini lighter out of her suitcase and put them into her purse. "I haven't even felt like a cigarette since I left home," she marvelled to herself.

"That's everything ready for tomorrow. Now it must be dinner time." She realised that she was starving. "I had so much food on the aeroplane, I don't know how I could possibly still be hungry!"

Half an hour later, she was seated at a corner booth in the restaurant. It was decorated in the same colour scheme as the rest of the motel. The same deep teal and browns in her room, in the reception and the bar. Paintings on the walls depicting old buildings she assumed were part of the local history. Buildings that were several hundreds of years old.

Stella smiled with excitement, this was real. She didn't have to pinch herself to believe it. She could feel the age, the ancient energy of a land with centuries of history. Generations of people, of spirits and ancestors, of magic and nature. Less than forty-eight hours ago, she had been sitting at home, and now here she was on the other side of the world.

"I had always hoped I would travel, but I never really believed it. And then, this. I wonder which came first, the magic or me believing in myself? Being magic, moving through portals, casting spells. Overseas travel, and tomorrow I am going to visit Stonehenge." The magic of the stones had intrigued Stella for as long as she could remember.

The two friends Stella had seen on the coach came in, they were still talking. They were obviously having a ball, enjoying the excitement of the trip. She could feel their energy, their connection and their excitement. She smiled, remembering the precious times she had spent with her friends, and in particular the connection she shared with Brigid and Maisie.

"Excuse me," the taller of the two women said as they stopped by her table. "Did I hear you tell the receptionist that you won a competition to be here?"

Stella beamed. "Yes I did. I still can't quite believe I am here."

"That is so wonderful. An amazing competition to win," the woman beamed back. "I think we saw you on our plane too. We have been planning this trip for a few years. My family came from Scotland, so we are going there after Stonehenge. Mag's family are from Prague, so we are also spending a week there. I'm Saz."

"It's so nice to meet you both. I'm Stella, from Queanbeyan, near Canberra. I am only here for a few days. After Stonehenge, there is another coach trip around London and then back home. It's my first time overseas. I am so excited."

"No way! Mags and I both live in Canberra too!"

"How exciting that your first time overseas and you get to see Stonehenge on the morning of the summer solstice."

Later that evening, Stella remembered every detail of the conversation. She marvelled at the synchronicity that she met two lovely women who lived close to where she lived. She snuggled under the crisp white covers, reciting the incantation she needed to use the next day.

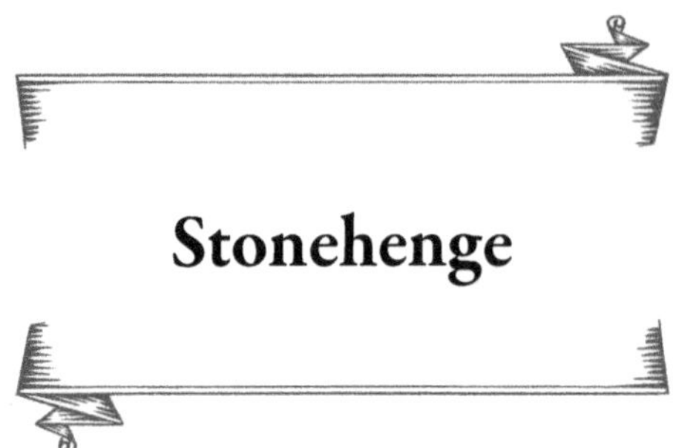

Stonehenge

L^{una}
Luna thought she would miss her simple, uncomplicated life.

"It is true. I do miss my cottage, Maud and Salem, and my plants," Luna thought. "But I love being back here with my coven."

"I missed this." Catherine hugged Luna. "Us hanging out in the workshop, making potions and lotions."

"Just like old times," Tizzie agreed.

The three felt the storm before they saw it. The clouds had an eerie green-grey colour, similar to the storm from so very long ago. Through the door of the workshop, loud claps of thunder and bright lightning filled the night sky. Heavy rain drops that felt flat and full and hot.

"I am pleased I am this side of the portal for this," Luna whispered to Catherine and Tizzie as the storm raged outside.

Stella

At four in the morning, Stella was handed a steaming hot cup of hot chocolate, a chocolate chip and banana muffin and a small bottle of black currant juice. As she slid into a seat on the coach, Mags and Saz jumped into the seat in front of her, juggling their breakfasts and their backpacks. It reminded Stella of a school bus trip to Sydney many years ago.

"STELLA! HELLO! HOW exciting!" Saz gave her a huge smile.

"Mags, Saz, hello! It is such an amazing day."

She marvelled at the fact that in the last couple of months, she had met and felt instantly drawn to Luna, Catherine, Tizzie, Brigid, Maisie, and now these two ladies, who lived only about half an hour away from where she lived now.

She grinned, feeling like a big kid and not like someone who was about to perform ancient magic inside a ring of mystical stones.

All three ladies watched out the window, their excitement growing the closer they got to Stonehenge. Stella whispered the words to the enchantment over and over. Even though she had memorised the words, she wanted to be focused for the spell.

Twenty people exited the bus, following the guide, listening to her history of the stones.

"Amazing!" Mags grabbed Stella's arm. "We have forty-five minutes to soak up the magic!"

"Definitely!" Stella responded. She would love to spend the time with her two new friends, but first, she had a job to do. How was she going to get away without being rude?

"Saz and I promised our families we would make a video of Stonehenge." Mags gave her a quick hug. "I hope you don't think we are being rude. We will come and find you after we have finished."

"Sounds like a plan," Stella replied, quietly marvelling at how synchronicity was becoming more an every day occurrence the more she was open to the possibilities of the unknown.

STONEHENGE WAS EVEN more magnificent and mystical in person than Stella imagined. The whole group appeared as mesmerised as she was. Some of them were huddled around the guide as she shared the history and mystery of the structure. She heard the guide talking about the science behind the mosses and lichen found on the stones and the unlikely scenarios that created the structure in the first place.

Over the years, people had sprayed Stonehenge with graffiti, they had carved their initials in the stones, taken tiny samples, people had even kissed the stones with lipstick. The scientific and spiritual information was fascinating. The trouble was Stella couldn't listen until after she had completed her task. She watched the horizon as the sun moved into position, aligned with the stones.

She moved over to the stones that led to the portal after a minor panic when she thought she was standing at the wrong part of the structure. No one, not even the guide, was paying her any attention. Mags and Saz were tucked away on the other side, creating their video adventure. Stella noted the multitude of guards positioned around the outside of the circle. The guide had explained that due to the continued vandalism over the years, there were guards twenty-four hours a day, seven days a week. There was a guard house where they took turns to rest, eat and get warm. Stella had read about how cold it got there in winter. She was glad she was visiting in midsummer.

Once she found the right place in the circle, she moved into position. Glancing around, she noted that Logan had been correct. From her position, she couldn't see anyone else, not even one guard. She hoped that meant they couldn't see her either.

Holding the pouch in her hands, she sprinkled the contents across the threshold. She could see the door, intuitively. No one started yelling at her, so she continued. She lit the candle and tucked it in the ground on the left-hand corner of the door. She was grateful that it wasn't windy. Stonehenge was on a small incline, out in the middle of an open field.

Stella knew the words off by heart. She spoke the enchantment three times as she had been instructed. As she stepped back from the portal, she heard the group gasp in wonder. The sunrise through the stones was magical and breathtaking. The colours were stronger than any sunrise she had ever seen. The sky changed from brilliant red, fading out pink and then orange, as the sun slowly rose into the clear morning sky. She gazed in silent wonder.

Mags and Saz came up behind Stella and gave her a huge hug. She hugged them back. She was more emotional than she thought she would be. Did she save the world? She wasn't sure. Maisie had said she wouldn't know until she got back home.

As she wandered through the circle with her new friends, she noticed a storm brewing to the east. The strangest storm she had ever seen. The grey-green cloud formation grew into a big tornado shape before it turned in on itself, and with a huge clap of thunder and lightning flash, it vanished.

Stella looked around the group. No one appeared to be looking in the direction of the storm. Knowing she would have to wait to find out what happened, she linked arms with Mags and Saz as they skipped back to the coach.

LUNA

Luna, Catherine and Tizzie were gathered at their coven in the woods. Their circle cast and their chants grew louder as the storm grew stronger.

In each realm, groups of three cast their spells. Chanting their incantations, using their symbols in their language as they lit their candles, set their crystal grids and burned their incense.

After one last big burst, the storm disappeared across all the realms.

Maiden mother crone,

You never have to be alone.

Be careful what you wish for and set your intentions with careful consideration.

Follow the cycles of the seasons, the phases of the moon.

Honour our feelings with our thoughts, actions and words.

Harm no one.

So mote it be.

After the Storm

Stella

"Never in my life had I imagined I would be spending two days seeing London from the top level of a double-decker bus!" Stella confided to one of the guides as they stopped outside Buckingham Palace on the afternoon of the first day. The majesty of the building and the guards in their huts on either side of the entry. The flag was flying on the top of the palace, which meant that King Charles was in residence.

Turning to admire the Queen Victoria Memorial directly opposite, Stella was struck by how fortunate she was. "Did I manifest this trip when I focused on winning the competition, or did I win the trip because of the magical intention that I had to save the world? I guess it really doesn't matter how it happened, I am going to enjoy every minute of it," Stella said to herself as she took more photos to show Andie and Emily when she got back home.

FINISHING LAST-MINUTE packing before the taxi ride to the airport, Stella glanced at her reflection in the mirror in the bathroom.

"Have I changed?" she mused. "I have travelled by myself to the other side of the world. I have met people I think can become good friends. I have witnessed ancient, mystical magic. People believe in me. So am I more confident?' Stella wondered. What changes will I make when I am home? Will I think, act and speak differently?" Stella had twenty-four hours to think about it during the trip home.

SHE HAD NO WAY OF CONTACTING her magic friends. She had not seen any storms since Stonehenge, which was positive. Brigid warned her not to try to cross over in her dreams while she was travelling. She would have to wait until she was home to know whether she had made a difference.

There was no way Stella would have tried to visit her friends in her dreams in the UK. Every night since she left home, her dreams were full of people. People whose faces were pressed right up to hers, right in front of her face. It was confronting the first time it happened. Stella got used to it and was intrigued watching the people come in and out of her vision. She wrote her dreams down in case they were important.

> *Knights in silver armour, a regiment of them, and some in single file, by themselves. Royalty, a king, I think, and a few princes. Then a magician or a mage, someone wise. Old crones in long flowing robes. Young children and youths, teenagers in rags. Lined up in front of an apothecary. They were all asking me for help. It is like I lived this life before.*

Luna

"It's been a couple days, and everything seems fine. Are you going to stay here now?" Catherine asked Luna.

"I miss my animal family, Salem and Maude." She put her arm around Catherine. "But when I am there, I miss you and Tizzie. I wish there was a way that I could travel back and forth easily."

Tizzie picked up the book she had been reading, "There may be a way," she whispered. "I have been looking at the books of our ancestors. They had a way of staying connected to their coven. We can link the tree at the back of your cottage to our workshop. We should be able to move back and forth freely. It is not exactly a portal, in that it will only work for those in the particular coven who creates it. This magic is limited to certain covens. In theory other magic folk could create portals to travel through realms, but they would need to be connected to someone in that other realm."

"Let's try it," Luna hugged her friends and walked over to the corner of the workshop.

She opened her eyes in her back garden. Salem ran to meet her, weaving between her legs, purring as loudly as an old farm tractor. Bert and Gert waved as they disappeared into the big tree.

"Thank you!" she called out, not sure if they heard her or not.

Luna scooped Salem into her arms and hugged him tight.

"Maude, breakfast!" The magpie was there before Luna had finished speaking, sitting on her perch, waiting for Luna to dig the seed out of the metal bin on the porch. Luna used to have the seed in a woven basket, but all the mice and other birds managed to get in and devour Maude's food. Neither crone nor bird were pleased with that.

As she swept out her cottage and the porch, it was like she had never gone away.

"Salem, I wish you could have come with me. Maybe you can one day."

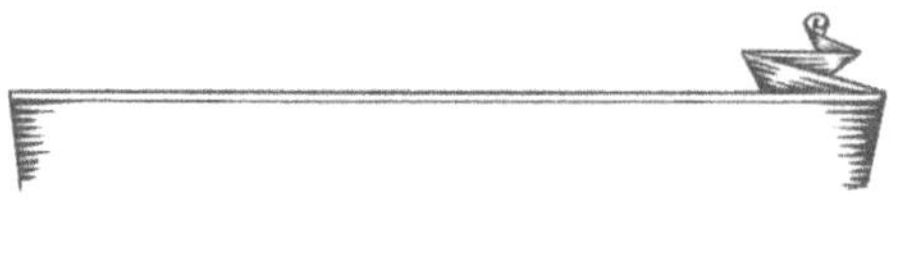

Home Sweet Home

Stella
Hopping out of the taxi, Stella thanked the driver and dropped her bags just inside her front door. She collected Puddles from her next-door neighbour, and ran down to the hedge. She closed her eyes and gently pushed the hedge. It didn't part like a velvet curtain. It felt prickly like a hedge was meant to. Puddles jumped down and wandered through the hedge. Stella held her breath. He returned a couple of seconds later.

"So now it is just a hedge?" Puddles snuggled back into her arms. Stella was happy that the incantation had worked. She was also a little sad that she couldn't use the portal to visit her coven. At least she could still visit them at night.

It was only nine o'clock in the morning. Stella hadn't slept on the plane.

"I'm going to wait until bedtime to sleep. That way, I can play with you, unpack everything and beat jet lag as well," Stella told her kitten as she opened the windows and doors to get fresh air circulating.

Later that afternoon, a knock on the front door distracted her just as she was starting to doze off. Emily and Andie walked in with a couple of pizza boxes and a tub of chocolate chip ice cream. "We thought you might have no food in the house, and we were hungry," Andie joked.

For Stella, having dinner with Emily and Andie was the best welcome home she could have asked for. She was so proud of the beautiful young women they were becoming. Both girls were so happy to see her and to hear all about her trip.

"Next time, win a trip for three," Emily asked with a smile as they hopped into the car to go home.

As she climbed into bed, she looked at her robe hanging on the door. With the portal closed, would she ever need to wear it again?

"Could I take my robe, my crystals and other things across in my dreams?" she asked Puddles. He looked up from his pillow at the end of the bed.

"You know what? I am going to try it." Stella put her robe on over her tracksuit, tucking a candle, her clear quartz and a sprig of rosemary into the pockets. She was almost asleep as she climbed into bed next to Puddles. As she drifted off, she focused on seeing Brigid and Maisie at the tavern.

"STELLA!" MAISIE AND Brigid embraced their friend. "You made it. We knew you would." Brigid handed her a tankard.

Stella took a sip. "Coffee!" she beamed at her friend.

"We figured you deserved it after saving the world," grinned Maisie.

"I am sure I didn't actually save the world, not by myself, at least." Stella grinned back.

"So what did I do? I mean, I know I closed the portals at Stonehenge. There was this crazy storm. It built up like a tornado, then it kind of imploded in on itself. Was that something we did?"

Brigid refilled Stella's mug, noting she had already drunk most of the coffee.

"We were successful. We closed the portals, keeping the magic where it was meant to be. We stopped the problem for now. The storm cloud was confirmation that it worked," Maisie said. "Magic is still growing, but there is no evidence of maliciousness."

"Thank goodness," Stella was relieved to hear that. "So how will we know if any new portals open?"

"We will notice a shift in the energies if that happens. Your world is too polluted, making it more difficult to feel the subtle changes," Brigid explained.

"We can teach you how to pick up on the changes in the energy field." Maisie offered.

"I see you figured out that you can use your robe to move things between worlds. Good work." Stella blushed at Brigid's praise.

"It was just something I was testing out," Stella confessed. "I have another question."

"Go ahead."

"I told you about the friends I made when I was on my trip?" Brigid and Maisie nodded.

"I get the impression that they might believe in magic. I felt a connection between us. Not the same as the connection I share with you. Can I be friends with them and still come here and spend time with you both? Can I be in two covens? Or doesn't it work like that?" This had been bothering Stella. She loved all her new friends, and she didn't want to have to choose one group.

Brigid responded, "Mags and Saz are interested in all sorts of witchy things. Like you, they thought magic was only in stories of faraway lands. Once they met you, the magic in them stirred. They don't know anything for certain yet. Their magic won't be as strong as yours, but they will be invaluable friends and your coven in your world.

"We will still be your coven too. You can visit as often as you would like to. We will teach you how to use your gifts and grow your magic," Brigid finished.

"Two covens, that is amazing." Stella was overjoyed.

BRIGID SMILED. "NOW it is time for you to go back to sleep. It has been a long week for you. There is nothing to worry about." The three women hugged as Stella slipped back into a deep sleep.

STELLA

"What do I tell Mags and Saz?" Stella wondered aloud. Puddles walked around her before settling into her lap. "If I told them everything that happened over the last few months, they would think I was crazy. But I can't really just tell them part of the story, it would make no sense. I guess I don't have to decide now. I am sure if they start playing with magic before I work out how to tell them, an elf or a fairy will help them."

"I'm a sprite!" Lexie appeared out of nowhere.

"Are you here all the time?"

"No way! I have better things to be doing. I was just passing through, and heard you talking to yourself." Lexie sat down in front of her. "There are others who will jump in and help your friends. You will teach them when you feel the time is right. Trust in you." Lexie disappeared as quickly as she arrived.

Focus on what we want, on where we want to go.
By the power of one and the power of three,
I call you to me, and me to you.
Together we see, we meet and share,
Harm to no one,
So mote it be.

Imbolc

It doesn't have to be true to feel true.
Luna

Imbolc is the halfway point between the winter solstice and the spring equinox is associated with new beginnings and the first stirrings of spring after the dark winter months. It is a time to light candles, plant seeds, and set intentions for the coming year. August was also her birth month. The days were slightly warmer, the plants were waking up. The feast honours Brigid, the goddess of fertility, fire, and healing.

Luna took her basket out into the garden to pick flowers to make a garland for the goddess. She placed the garland on her altar.

Stella

Spending time with her new friends, and learning about magic, Stella was enjoying life for the first time in a long time. Stella decided that, for now, it was time for her to focus on herself and her magic. Hearing the postman, she skipped to the mailbox.

Opening the letter that didn't look like a bill, Stella had to read the letter twice for the words to sink in. Mrs K, her friend, had passed away unexpectedly from a short respiratory illness. Stella blinked back the tears. She had been meaning to visit Mrs K after she returned from her trip to Scotland.

She had grown attached to the elegant elderly lady. They had met at the library at her children's primary school ten years ago and had instantly become friends.

The letter went on to say that Mrs K had named Stella as next of kin and left Stella her house. The women had formed a strong bond, a shared love of books and writing, and for most of the last five years, they had met at least once a month for coffee. She knew Mrs K had no children of her own and had often said Stella was like the daughter she had never had. The letter gave her the details of who she had to contact and what she had to do.

Three days later, she unlocked the door to the house that was going to become her home. She was struck that they had very similar tastes in home décor. "A kindred soul," she muttered.

Her solicitor had said the house, all its belongings and everything in the garden were all hers now. He had explained that Stella didn't have to keep everything and that she could have a garage sale or donate Mrs K's belongings to a local charity.

As she wandered from room to room, there really wasn't anything she would change. She loved the colourful feature walls, green in the kitchen, blue in the living area, and purple in the master bedroom. The wooden floors throughout reminded her of her childhood home. Real floorboards, not vinyl. Stella had left the home she shared with her ex-husband and the children, with little more than her clothes. She had managed to collect some second-hand furniture from the local op shop. Mrs K's furniture choices were simple. Pine and white. Books lined the walls of one spare room, set up as a writer's nook.

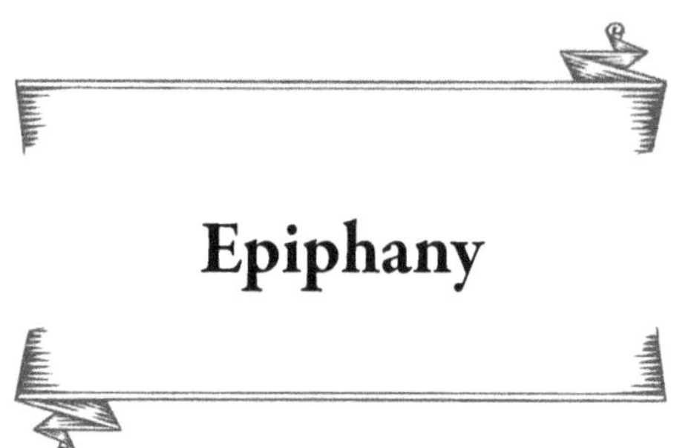

Epiphany

Luna

Being a witch was an interesting journey. Some days Luna remembered things she had not previously known. The ingredients to add into a cinnamon simmer pot, or how to make compost for growing mushrooms. Both are handy things to know on the farm. Other more obscure knowledge was also handy and a constant source of amazement to the seasoned witch. Runes and how to use them, what each of the little symbols meant, and how runes themselves can be a useful divination tool. Luna had made her own set of runes from stones found in the stream at the bottom of her garden.

On other days the witch seemed to forget things she thought she had known forever. Was it easier to remember or was it better to forget? Which truth was real? Witch or crazy old lady? Did it have to be one or the other?

But don't be fooled. Beneath the eccentric exterior lay a powerful witch. A crone who had many years of skills and experience, and she remembered every single spell and enchantment she had ever cast.

Stella

Stella was just as powerful. Her magic was a natural progression to the spiritual path she had been traveling for years. Lighting candles and incense. Making her own candles. Placing crystals and candles and photos together on a shelf. Collecting and drying herbs. Collecting jars. Setting intentions, affirmation and mindfulness. Meditations. With all these tools, she had been unknowingly growing her craft.

It all came to a head on that summer solstice morning. Across realms and time zones. Witches three times three got the job done.

STELLA WAS PLEASED to be so close to finishing her story notes. It had been more difficult than she had imagined, putting pen to paper and telling her version of the rift. She hoped her children would read it, but she also hoped her tragedy would help save others from a similar life of mistakes and regret.

Since visiting Stonehenge, Stella had a much lighter and brighter view of the world. Her trips through the portal to another realm had a profound effect on her. Her ability to perform magic, to control some of the elements around her, had changed her. Meeting people who believed in her and loved her for who she was had boosted her confidence. She was driven to finish her story, to write a version that aligned with who she was now.

"When I started putting my thoughts down on paper, I thought I knew how this book was going to end. I no longer held on to the anger and grief I was holding on to when I wrote the book the first time. But I was still frustrated and incredibly sad, knowing that I had to shoulder half the blame for what failed. I wanted to document it for my children to read. To write about my experiences, to help others." Stella was rehearsing what she would say if she was asked about her book.

"AS I BEGAN TO WRITE, I discovered a few interesting truths. The most significant being that it doesn't have to be true to feel true. I focused on getting my point of view across to be understood. Their views and memories are just as important and valid as mine.

"The other truth I stumbled across is that releasing and letting go of baggage is an ongoing process. We continually re-evaluate and release what no longer serves us. We use our baggage as stepping stones, placed under our feet, to lift us higher."

As she paused, Puddles came over and jumped up into her lap. She continued her train of thought.

"Another uncomfortable truth is that there may not be a happy ending, no matter how hard I wish for it. My dream for my children is for them to be happy as they find their place in the world."

Luna

Luna never tired of sitting outside, in front of a fire, as the flames grew and waned, snapping and crackling. A fire was also the best tool to dispose of rubbish. Easier than a drive to the local waste centre. There was no weekly bin collection out here.

Tonight she was going to meet Catherine and Tizzie in the flames. Their friendship rekindled. They were weaving magic like in the old days. Luna was worried that if she moved through the tree behind her cottage, she would once again want to stay with her friends.

Spells and the magic power of three. Three witches in the coven. Chants repeated three times three.

Three times three.

The magic power of three.

Across realms and lifetimes,

I call thee to me,

May we chant and dance once again.

So mote it be.

New Friendships

Stella

Stella was so pleased she had met Saz and Mags, and now when she found out they lived less than thirty minutes from where she worked and less than twenty minutes from Mrs K's house, her new home.

The magic power of three.

She had no idea what to wear to a coven meeting. To be honest, she didn't even know if Mags and Saz had invited her to a coven to celebrate the Spring Equinox or if it was an invitation to tea and biscuits. She felt energised by the events of the last few months. She saw magic in everything. She felt the energy of nature everywhere.

"It is far more likely that this was just a get-together to talk about their trip and get to know each other," Stella told Puddles and Harry.

After changing her outfit several times, she settled on blue jean leggings and a purple gypsy shirt. With black sneakers, her witchy medallion and hoop earrings.

Stella said goodbye to Puddles and Harry, who had both easily settled into life in their new home. Today Puddles was acting a little strangely. He kept walking past the cupboard in the spare room, where Stella was settling up her office and her altar.

"What is it Puddles? What's wrong?" She picked him up and opened the cupboard doors. The shelves she had already filled with books, candles, essential oils and other knick-knacks. The left side, the hanging section, was where Stella kept her purple coat and her robes.

Stella blinked. A light was shining from behind her coat, behind the back of the cupboard.

"It can't be, can it?" she asked Puddles, instinctively knowing the answer.

"Okay come on, just for a minute." She closed her eyes and walked through the back of the cupboard. When she opened her eyes, she was looking at another field, with an old farmhouse in front of her. Feeling Puddles squirm in her arms, trying to get down, and remembering she was supposed to be visiting her new friends, she turned and walked back through the cupboard.

"When I come home," she told Puddles. "I don't want to miss afternoon tea."

She shut the cupboard door and the door of the room. She didn't want Puddles to accidentally wander into the portal.

"What does this mean? Why is there a portal at the back of my cupboard?" Her head was filled with questions as to why magic was back as she drove to Mag's house.

"WE ARE SO GLAD YOU came," Mags opened the door. "Come out to the verandah, and say hi to Saz."

As Stella walked through Mag's house, she noticed the walls were painted a soft blue. She loved the way the pine furniture complemented the blue and white paint, the darker blue curtains and the cream-tiled floors.

Outside, the verandah was just as pretty. Wooden decking and an old comfy sofa draped with a colourful crochet square rug. Saz was sitting at a glass-topped outdoor table on one of four grey rattan-style chairs. The table was set with an owl teapot, three matching mugs, and a vase of pink and yellow roses. A cake stand filled with tiny cupcakes sat on one side of the rectangular table. The cupcakes looked exquisite, iced with such pretty pastel colours and little sparkly flowers and stars sprinkled on the top.

STELLA MADE A NOTE to remember to compliment whoever made them.

Along the wall, under the window, was an altar. An elegant witch sitting on her broomstick, a rose quartz tower point, a mini cauldron full of lovely smelling herbs and a candelabra of white pillar candles. She felt her heart jump. Lots of people have altars like that and aren't magical or aren't aware that they are magical. It was more likely that they loved the witchy hippy things, just like she did.

Stella placed the banana cake she made on the table next to the cupcake stand.

Saz jumped up and hugged Stella. "Hello!"

Stella instantly felt at home, as if she had known these women for years instead of weeks.

"Sit down, tell us how the rest of your whirlwind trip went. Ours was so wonderful that we are planning our next trip already. Do you want to come too?" Stella was getting used to the way Saz talked a hundred miles an hour, sometimes about several topics all at once.

"Give the girl a chance to sit down and have a sip of her tea," Mags admonished her friend. Turning to Stella she added, "I hope tea is okay. I can make you a coffee instead."

Stella smiled, "Tea is fine, thank you, and thank you for inviting me. Those cupcakes look amazing! Mine always end up looking wonky, but those would win a competition!"

Mags blushed, "I love baking. I have been making those since I was six years old."

Saz passed the cupcakes to Stella. The three ladies each munched on a dainty treat, iced with sugary sparkly icing, sipping their cups of peppermint tea.

GLANCING AT MAGS, SAZ asked Stella, "Have you ever watched the television show Charmed?" Mags rolled her eyes.

"Yes. I love that show! Although I have only seen some episodes. I don't have a television anymore."

"Mags has the boxed set. We have watched it all the way through at least twice now, I think." Saz clapped her hands together. "We love that show. We could schedule a date to watch it together. We wouldn't mind watching it again, would we, Mags?" Without waiting for an answer, she continued.

"When we first met at the motel before we visited Stonehenge, both Mags and I felt like we already knew you, like we were all best friends."

Stella nodded, "I felt the same, like we were connected somehow."

"We almost invited you to come with us to Europe," Saz confided, "But Mags said that would be too weird. How was the rest of your trip?"

"Absolutely amazing! I saw Buckingham Palace, Big Ben, London Bridge, Westminster Abbey, Trafalgar Square, and Piccadilly Circus, all from the top of a red double-decker bus. It still feels like a dream. A wonderful delicious dream." Stella paused, stopping herself before she said too much and shared her magical secret.

"I am so glad you enjoyed it." Mags smiled. "Our trip was amazing too. We had been planning it for a while. It was only when my dad surprised me with the plane tickets that we realised we could make it to Stonehenge for the summer solstice. It all fell into place from there."

"SYNCHRONICITY," SAZ murmured.

"Yes!" Stella continued, "I entered the competition in an obscure online magazine I found. I had just read about manifestation, so I applied what I had learnt. I feel like I believed it enough that it came true." She paused, looking at both her new friends for signs they thought she was crazy.

Saz glanced at Mags and blurted out, "Mags and I, well, we want to be witches, like in Charmed. We collect herbs, we use crystals and essential oils. We practise spells and enchantments, and we meet up during the witchy celebrations. Well, we meet up every day, but we also meet and practise witchy stuff." Saz jumped as she was speaking, nearly knocking over the cupcakes.

"Saz!" Mags cautioned her friend. "If you spill those, all I have left in the fridge is apples and strawberries."

"I have a confession to make," Stella spoke up. "When you invited me over, I kept thinking you were inviting me to a coven meeting. It is like the three of us communicate without speaking."

"Telepathically," Mags confirmed. "At least that's how we think of it. We can tell each other things without talking or even being in the same room."

"So I am not going crazy," Stella thought to herself.

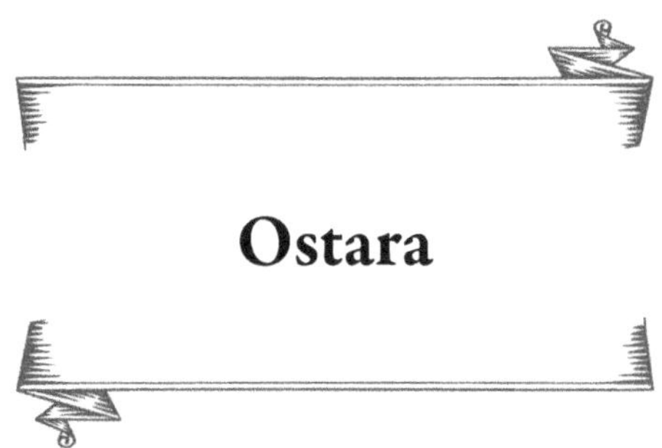

Ostara

S tella
The afternoon turned into a celebration of Ostara, the spring equinox. Stella, Mags and Saz celebrated new life, Ostara the German goddess of fertility and new beginnings. They collected flowers and made flower garlands from the daisies, geraniums and azaleas growing in big pots on the verandah.

It seemed like only an hour had passed, but the moon was already peeping over the horizon by the time Stella left, promising to plan another get together soon. The moon was full of vibrating energy. Stella felt it in every fibre of her body, as she drove home, the moon right in front of her windscreen, showing her the way home.

AT HOME, SNUGGLING with Puddles, Stella thought back over the day. She enjoyed her afternoon with her new friends, her new coven. "I am already planning the next afternoon together. We can meet here, I'll show them some of the magic I am learning. It will be so much fun." She hopped out of bed.

"Today we drank peppermint tea, ate tiny cupcakes, and watched Charmed. It was a wonderful afternoon," she told Puddles, smiling at the memory.

Suddenly Stella remembered the portal. Puddles looked up at Stella.

"You stay there Puddles. I will be back soon." She shut the spare room door to stop her kitten from following her, opened the cupboard, and put on her robes. She then walked through the portal with her eyes closed.

She opened her eyes to the most spectacular sunset she had ever seen. The sky was a brilliant red, with shades of pink, oranges and yellow. She saw the farmhouse she had seen earlier, some paddocks with a crop she didn't recognise, and a woody forest off to the left. In the fields in between, she could see some highland cattle.

A horse-drawn wagon came into view.

"Come and join us Stella! We are going to celebrate the Spring Equinox."

Luna

Luna decorated eggs and collected flowers. She had an old statue of a rabbit she had owned for many years. Each year on Ostara, she would bring him into the front garden of daisies and geraniums in honour of the goddess. As she was putting together her spring garland, she felt a couple of drops of rain.

The first rain of the spring contains special luck-drawing powers, even more so if it coincides with the spring equinox. Luna raced inside, as fast as her old legs would carry her, to grab a jar to collect the water. It was a good thing her wardrobe choices were thick black leggings rather than the traditional witchy long black flowing robes. She was much less likely to trip over wearing leggings. Without agonising over which jar was best, as she would usually do, she grabbed the biggest empty glass jar she could find.

With any luck, she would be able to collect enough to use for a quick wash. Using the first spring rainwater for bathing would bring a year of luck, love and joy, youth, romance and fertility. Sprinkling her altar and magic tools for extra powers when casting spells.

She placed the jar on the outdoor table. There were no plants or trees or parts of her cottage that would stop the jar from filling with the rain. The crone set an intention for a season of good luck and a blessing for the much-needed rain for her garden. Next, the crone picked some basil, tucking the sprigs into a small pot of dirt, and placed it next to the jar.

"Thank you," she whispered to her basil bush, cutting only as much of the plant as she needed for her intention, "for sharing your leaves and flowers so I may set my intentions for abundance and prosperity." Luna remembered reading that adding basil to the rainwater and washing her face, hands and feet in the water helps to attract abundance. Over the years, this practice had provided mixed results. Increased sales of her book, gifts of plants, and other gifts and opportunities. Luna settled in on her rocking chair and watched the rain from the shelter of her front porch.

Stella

Stella ran over and hopped on the end of the wagon with Brigid and Maisie. She was so used to strange things happening she didn't even question how or why they just happened to be driving past on the back of a wagon, just at the right time to spot her as she came through the portal.

"When did the portal open? How many others opened? Why did it open? Where are we going? How awesome to see you!" Stella's words tumbled out as the wagon pulled up in a big field where a large bonfire was burning, lighting up the evening sky. She stared at the scene in front of her in delight. About thirty people were celebrating the spring festival, singing and chanting as they danced around the flames.

Brigid smiled as they hugged. "We don't know why the portals are opening again. We are on our way to our spring festival. We are so glad you can join us."

"Did another portal open up in your world, or did you use your portal spell?" Maisie asked, making room for Stella on the back of the wagon.

"A portal in the cupboard in the spare bedroom in my new house." Stella pointed to the lightning on the horizon. "Is that the start of another storm because the portals are opening again?"

Brigid nodded. "We think they must be. We have heard about a couple of portals opening here, and now in your world. Logan has spoken to some of his contacts in the other realms. They haven't seen any storms or portals opening again yet. So far, the portals are only in your world and ours."

"Luna thinks there may be someone else in your world who has discovered magic," Maisie added. "We can feel the energy of discovery and new magic. You are the only person we have seen cross over here. It doesn't make a lot of sense yet. I am sure we will find out more in time."

"Do you think it could be because Mags and Saz have been practicing their magic more since they returned from Stonehenge? I had tea with them today. They are energised by the idea of magic and want to learn everything they can. I didn't tell them anything about all this. The three of us share a connection that is nearly as strong as the connection I have with the two of you." Stella paused before asking, "Did I do the right thing? By not telling them, I mean."

"If their energies are growing stronger and they are connected to you, then yes that would explain the portals opening between here and your world." Brigid paused as a youth twirling some fire sticks danced past, whooping and yelling, playing up to the gathering.

A group of children dressed as flower spirits danced past, giggling as they imitated the fire twirler. About ten women sitting around the fire kept a watchful eye on their children. The men in the group were building an image of the goddess out of sticks and branches.

"If their magic is growing and your connection is strong, you will need to guide them through their lessons," Maisie said. "They don't have your strength or power. They will need to be taught."

"If they were to go through a portal, I am not sure where they would end up," Brigid mused. "It would be this realm, but not here or at this time period."

"How do you feel about teaching them? From your book?" Maisie asked as the bonfire crackled and hissed, sending an eerie light out in the darkness.

Stella thought about the question for a moment before answering, "I could do it. I would like to. It makes sense that I teach them. Even though I am fairly new to this, it feels like knowledge I have always had. Like the information has always been there. I just couldn't access it. Until now. Can I bring them through the portal in my house to you or the tavern, so they can meet you both?" she asked.

"Not yet. We don't know how stable these portals are. When we go back home, we will tell Luna and Logan and their covens that we met you and what we discussed. Blair and Angus can test the stability of the portals using a technology they learnt from your world." Brigid said as she felt in the pocket of her robes and pulled out a piece of paper. She handed the paper to Stella. "Before you tell Mags and Saz your story, cast a circle using this chant. It will keep your words between the three of you. A pact that can't be broken. Not because we think they can't be trusted, but because we never know when others are listening."

"If you have a collection of crystals or trinkets, choose one for Mags and one for Saz," Maisie said as she pointed to the bracelet she had given Stella before her trip. "It is a way of staying connected. A shared bond."

Stella nodded. "I have the perfect crystal for each of them and a couple of other trinkets I have collected."

"We should go back now, the celebration is nearly over," Maisie pointed out as the bonfire slowly faded out. Seeing Stella's quizzical look, she added, "Yes, that was magic. We don't leave fires burning in case they get out of control and destroy the surrounding forest or farms."

"We will drop you back at your portal," Brigid offered as they walked back to the wagon that was waiting for them. Most of the crowd had already disappeared. Some were hopping into wagons, and others were walking towards the woods. A couple were on horses, heading towards the farmhouses in the distance.

"We will see you soon. You can focus the portal so that it brings you to the tavern. Like you did before. If you want help with Mags and Saz come and see us," Brigid said.

"Come and see us anyway, and anytime," Maisie added, looking at Brigid. "That is what she means."

"I know that." Stella smiled at them both. "I will visit soon, I promise."

The Reveal

S tella

The next morning, Stella found an old stationery set she had kept for at least twenty years in case she ever needed it. It reminded her of being a kid at home, writing invitations and thank you letters. Before the internet, even before computers. When all mail was snail mail.

Using her best handwriting, she wrote out two invitations, one for Saz and one for Mags, to join her to celebrate her new home. She decorated the floral stationery with stickers, addressed the envelopes and dropped them into the post box on her way to work. "It's lucky I keep spare stamps here just in case," she told Puddles as she stuck the stamps on the envelopes. "It is much easier than having to line up at the post office just to buy a couple."

SATURDAY WAS THE DAY. Stella was feeling nervous and excited. She had never spoken about her experiences with magic to anyone. Up before dawn, she had cleaned her new home from top to bottom.

"Time to go outside in the garden," she told Puddles as she put on his lead. "The biscuits and cakes are cooling on the racks. They won't be here for a couple of hours, and I need a distraction." Puddles loved being outside and even put up with the lead and harness if it meant he could spend more time with Stella.

She had brought her potted plants from her rental. Instead of transplanting them into her garden, she had arranged the geraniums and roses on the front verandah to welcome everyone who came to the door. The pots of peppermint and lavender were on the back verandah alongside the lemongrass, thyme and rosemary that Mrs K had growing in her kitchen garden. Mrs K even had a little greenhouse full of pots and a box full of seeds. Stella was trying her skill at growing plants from seeds with mixed results.

"I am much better at growing plants from cuttings," she said as Puddles watched her planting out the geraniums she had been growing in the greenhouse. "Some days, I still feel like this is a dream. I have my own home and my own garden. Apart from wanting my kids to visit, and Andie and Emily do now, the one other thing that I love is my garden. It is my haven and my happy place."

"Still talking to yourself, I see." Lexie walked out from under the elephant ear plant.

Stella smiled. "Of course!"

"Are you nervous about today?"

Stella looked at the sprite. "How do you know? Of course, you know." Stella sat down next to the sprite, holding Puddles in case he decided to get too close to Lexie. "I am a little nervous, but I trust I will work out what to say."

"Yes, you will. You have changed. You believe in yourself more now than when we first met." Lexie stood up and walked to the back of the garden bed. "I will be here if you need me, but I don't think you will." She waved goodbye as she went back through the garden.

AS STELLA SET THE TABLE before her guests arrived, she felt a shift in the energy around her. Everything seemed to be infused with magic. She worked out how she would share her story with her new friends. She took a couple of deep breaths in and out, centring and focusing her energy.

"Your home is beautiful," said Mags as Stella led them through to the table on the back verandah.

"It is just how I imagined it would be," Saz said breathlessly, in that excited little girl voice she used when she was happy.

"Thank you," replied Stella. "And thank you both for coming. Please sit down."

"Now before we have our tea and cake, I want to share something with you." Stella's heart was pounding in her chest as she continued, "I wanted to give you each a gift," She passed each lady a little purple organza bag. Mags' bag held a lapis lazuli crystal and a little key charm. Saz's bag held a little pentagram and a sodalite crystal.

"The crystals and charms will keep you safe and protected. We will be connected too when you wear them or carry them with you." Stella showed the ladies her necklace with the key and the amethyst. "The key on my necklace was given to me by someone who has taught me a lot, about magic and mystical aspects of life. I am connected to her and her world through the key, and this bracelet, infused with positive intentions."

"What I am trying to say," Stella continued as both Mags and Saz listened attentively, holding their presents in their hands. "Is that magic is real. It is about mindfulness, a positive mindset, creativity and setting intentions, as well as the witchy tools like crystals, talismans, sigils, spells, herbs, oils, portals, dreams and more, so much more. Not so long ago I was like you. I dabbled in using these tools, lighting candles, setting intentions, but I didn't believe in myself. I didn't believe I was magic. Now I can perform magic, not like a magician in a show or a circus. I can make things happen. I can teach you both. To make candle flames change direction, to create a ball of energy or an invisibility cloak." Stella stopped, gauging her friend's reactions before saying any more.

"For me, it is about being attuned to the natural world," Mags said, "Using herbs and essential oils for healing, eating healthy foods. Healing with my hands. Using Reiki and healing using my energy. I have been able to do that for as long as I can remember. I suppose that is part of being magic, now that we are talking about it."

Stella nodded. "I agree. Magic is about concentrating, using our strengths to make positive changes."

"I feel spirits, I hear voices, and I see people's auras. I can tell if they are sick or sad. If people are in danger, I see it before it happens." Saz spoke softly.

"We can share our gifts, teaching each other, if we want to and feel safe to do so," Stella told her friends.

"A few months ago I found a portal in the bottom of the garden of the rental property I was living in. It took me to another time and place. I met people for whom magic was part of daily life. I have also met other magical creatures, fairies and sprites. I can travel in my dreams to other realms. It does sound crazy," she acknowledged.

"I dream too. In my dreams, I am in medieval times, in Scotland or England somewhere with other women. It feels like we have been friends forever. Like with you, Stella," Saz said.

"I have similar dreams of being in a coven," Mags agreed.

Stella grinned to herself. She thought it might have been difficult to talk about. Instead it was the most natural conversation in the world. She stood up, smiling at her guests. "I think it is time for a cuppa and some cakes."

A moment of understanding is worth a thousand words,
Even if it is only heard by one,
The power of one,
The power of intentions,
The power of the cycles of the seasons and of being magical creatures ,
The power of three, three chants, three dances, three intentions,
Joining together as one,
So mote it be.

Things Change

S tella

Morning time was the best time. A brand new day full of endless possibilities. To set intentions while stirring her cup of peppermint tea always made Stella feel so wonderfully magic. She used this time to focus her thoughts and actions for the day. Yesterday had gone so very well. Mags and Stella had stayed for most of the day. After their cups of tea and biscuits, they had spent some time in the garden. They had agreed to meet again the following weekend at Stella's. Mags was going to teach them how to make delicate moon crescent pastries, Saz was going to share how to craft spell pouches and gift sets and Stella was going to show them some herbs that were good for eating and wellbeing. There was even talk of a sleepover if Mags brought over their Charmed DVDs.

Luna

Ever since she returned to her cottage, Luna felt out of place. She missed her friends, but it was more than that. The crone had chosen to stay in her world rather than with her coven because she was scared of her power. She had never admitted this to anyone, but since she lost her children, it was easier to hide and pretend to be crazy than to face her power.

"I don't know where I belong anymore," she told Salem and Maude one morning. "I don't even feel like working in my garden. I need a sign to tell me what is the right move." The crone looked around as if she expected someone to jump out at her and provide her the solution.

"I wish I could pick up my cottage and take it through the portal. With you both as well. I think I want to be with Tizzie and Catherine. With the portals open again, they might need me. I think I need them too. I think I need to practice magic again. I have been hiding far too long."

Broomhilda

Broomhilda was very glad to hear Luna's wishes. It was time for Luna to move back through the portal and spend time with her coven. She needed to remember who she was. Being a fairy, Broomhilda probably could wave her magic wand and move Luna and her cottage from one land to another. That would upset the natural order of things. Broomhilda watched to see what would happen next.

Luna

As Luna swept her path, she saw a young lady walking down the path towards her. This was an unusual occurrence. Luna couldn't help but wonder if this was an answer to her question.

"Excuse me," the visitor said, approaching Luna. "I know this will sound like an unusual request, but is there any chance this cottage is for rent? I am a writer, and I am looking for somewhere secluded to stay while I write my book. I saw your cottage from the road, and I fell in love with the place. My name is Annie." Annie put out her hand to shake the crone's hand.

"I'M LUNA. WHAT SORT of books do you write?" Luna tried to sound calm whilst her mind was racing. "Could this be my Annie?" she thought, trying not to stare. "She is about the right age."

"I am writing a series of books about witches. Totally fiction, of course. When I was a child, I used to dream about a world where witches and wizards were real. Now that I am grown up, I still sometimes have the same dreams. I decided to write them down. To make them into children's books. My brother Fred will help me illustrate and publish them. The thing is, I have to have them finished in six months." Annie handed Luna a business card. "I didn't mean to come in and sound like I expected you to rent me your home." She said apologetically. "My telephone number, in case you know of any other places like this cottage that I could rent." Annie stopped. " I don't normally talk so much. I am sorry I disturbed you."

As Annie started to leave, Luna crossed her fingers and called out after her. "This cottage is for rent. For six months as it happens."

"Really? Oh, that's wonderful." Annie clasped her hands together in excitement.

Luna wanted to hug this lady, who she was almost certain was her daughter, yet something told her to wait. For now, it was enough to know that her children might be alive and okay.

"Do you live near here?" Luna wanted to keep Annie talking as long as she could while she processed what was happening.

"At the moment, I live in Brisbane, but I really want to write the books somewhere out here. I was drawn to this area. It would only be for six months. When were you planning to rent this out? And how much?" Annie enquired.

Thinking quickly, Luna replied, "I am actually keen for someone to house sit or cottage sit. I don't really want any money. I have a kitten and a magpie I would like looked after as well. Would you be interested in staying here and house-sitting and pet-sitting? If so, would tomorrow be too soon?"

"Oh my goodness," Annie replied. "That sounds just perfect. I will take good care of your cottage and your pets, I promise. May I ask where you are going for six months?"

"I promised to visit my sisters. They live in Scotland. My flight leaves tomorrow evening. I was getting worried that maybe I would have to give away my kitten as I couldn't find anyone to house-sit." Luna grinned. "Perfect timing."

"I agree." Annie smiled back at Luna, who was more convinced than ever that she was talking to her eldest daughter. "I'd better go home and pack. If I am back tomorrow morning, before lunch, would that work?"

"That would be perfect," Luna responded, trying to decide whether it would be inappropriate to give Annie a hug. Before she could decide, Annie hugged Luna before skipping down the path where she came from, calling out, "I'll see you tomorrow!"

Luna sat down on her rocking chair on the front porch. "I didn't dream that did I?" Salem jumped up on the crone's lap, snuggling in. "My precious Salem. I won't be gone forever, I promise. Annie will take good care of you. I just know she will." Patting Salem, Luna marvelled at the synchronicity of her life.

ANNIE HAD THE SAME olive skin, dark brown hair and deep brown eyes that Luna remembered when she thought of her eldest daughter. That mischievous spirit, that sense of fun and adventure. Not being afraid to bounce up the path to the door of a stranger to ask if their cottage was available. "There is hope for a life full of dreams coming true. I am certain of that now. I am not imagining it. A mother can tell. Every cell in my body is telling me that is my daughter," she whispered to Salem excitedly. "Can you feel it? That positive energy, swirling around us. The connection between our worlds is strengthening. It is time for change, positive change."

Luna read the words she had written on the back of the photo of her children, all those years ago.

Bring more magic to my day,
Take all my fears, cares and worries away,
Make me sparkly, make me bright, Fill my day with love and light,
Beauty and love reveal to me,
Luck and joy make me feel free,
Surprise, success and harmony,
I welcome thee to surround me,
This is my will,
So mote it be.

Gratitude

Gratitude is one of the healthiest of our human emotions. The more we express gratitude for what we have, the more likely we will find even more to express gratitude for.

Luna

Luna loved the energy of the new moon.

She also loved the night before the new moon, the dark moon.

It reminded the crone of everyone turning off all their electrical appliances once a year for Earth Hour. To Luna, it was a time to unplug and reset.

A time when the earth, the heavens and the sea were able to breathe a collective sigh and relax under the dark sky. For the crone, sleeping less the older she got, she found the dark moon was the best night of the month for sleep.

The new moon's energy was exciting, refreshing and rejuvenating. During the new moon phase, the crone's dreams were lighter and more creative. She was more in tune with her spell work. She created candles, essential oil blends, broomsticks and witches' bells. She would use the herbs she had dried in teas, infusions and tinctures. She loved repurposing jars and bottles, even the labels she made from paper she had created from paper scraps.

There was no waste or rubbish in this witch's home. The two weeks after the new moon was a time of positive emotions, planning and spell-making. Gratitude for all the knowledge of the witch. Gratitude for both her past and present.

Sitting out on the chilly spring evening after the warm spring day, Luna wrapped her shawl around her shoulders. She loved the shawl, crocheted by her sister a long time ago.

The crone's fire pit was a crooked circle of stones. Rocks she had handpicked from the caves around the farm cottage. She had painstakingly chosen a variety of stones, grey or brown, jagged and smooth, odd sizes and the perfect size to keep this witch warm when moon gazing. It had taken her a few weeks, but she had placed each one in a circle, in the best place for moon gazing.

During each day in the garden, Luna would find sticks, twigs and branches and pile them up beside the fire pit. Pine cones too. Pine cones are perfect on a raging fire. Such an awesome aroma, a comforting warmth almost impossible to describe.

Tonight there was no time for lighting a fire. The crone made sure there was enough firewood there if Annie wanted to light a fire while she stayed at the cottage. Luna was grateful that she didn't collect stuff. She did make sure the floors, shelves and furniture were clean and tidy. She tucked most of her witchy things into the chest under the window. She kept candles and crystals on her altar. And one of the photos she had of her children from so long ago. She was taking some photos with her and a change of clothes. Everything else she needed, she would find as she needed it.

Was Annie her daughter? She suspected she would find out soon enough. She looked around her cottage, checking to see if there was anything else that needed doing before she left. Satisfied that everything was in order, Luna climbed into bed with Salem tucked up on his blanket next to her.

STELLA

Stella looked at her new fire pit. She liked the way the metal was twisted into random shapes to imitate flames rising from an open fire. She had picked it up, second-hand from a garage sale around the corner. It wasn't too bad, dragging it home, even up the hill. It was such a short distance to drag it for the possibility of having a wood fire under the light of the moon. Or during the night of the dark moon.

She used to hate the dark. It was crazy for a witch to be scared of the dark. It is more accurate to say that she didn't like not being able to see clearly in the dark. That feeling of not being in control. Stella remembered that feeling of claustrophobia, similar to the agoraphobia that she felt so often in shopping centres.

"It all makes sense now that I am remembering some of who I was in the past," Stella told Puddles, who was sitting with her by the fire pit.

"I remember being a young kid, trapped in a trunk. I was hiding in the back of a carriage. At least I don't fear the dark anymore. Also I am learning more about me, and what magic can do."

The voices and spirits that whispered to her were friendly enough. They might suggest she take a different road to work. To leave for work five minutes later. To make contact with a family member or friend. Every single time that she heeded the words, she found something to be grateful for.

It was time to test out the fire pit. She had never lit a fire before, and she spent an hour or so trying to convince herself she could do it. She didn't even think about using magic to start it.

"I HAVE BEEN GATHERING sticks and twigs for weeks. I even bought a bag of firewood, so I can make sure I can light this fire before I treat the kids to roasting marshmallows."

"Maybe I should start burning some paper first," she told Puddles.

"You can do this," whispered her spirit guide. Stella looked around, half expecting to see Lexie, but she knew that sprites didn't like leaving their home once the sun went down.

"You've got this."

It took half an hour, but eventually, Stella was sitting in the camp chair with a cup of tea in her hand, watching the flames dance and bounce around on the sticks in her fire pit.

"I did it!"

Sitting outside on the night before the new moon, Stella learnt something important. She learnt that she could do important stuff like lighting a fire, which was a very useful skill on so many levels. It would certainly have been useful in her previous existence, back in medieval times.

A couple of green tree frogs jumped up to her chair.

"Hey little fellas, do you like the fire I made?"

After a few minutes, the frogs jumped back out of sight. Out of the light and away from the owls. Stella hadn't seen the owls yet, but she knew they were there. Some nights she lay awake and listened to the jump, jump, jump of the green tree frogs, followed by a thud as an owl swooped down and grabbed one from the roof for a late-night snack.

THE CIRCLE OF LIFE.

Gratitude, real gratitude, is not Pollyanna sayings, trite unicorns, balloons and fairyfloss. Real gratitude is finding the moments in the everyday that makes us smile. Gratitude for a warm bed, enough food, family and friends.

We can also be grateful for things that haven't yet happened.

Gratitude for things we want to manifest in our lives.

Believing with all our mind, body, heart and soul that our dreams can come true? Now that is a skill worth learning.

"For me, learning magic is about learning to control our energies and feelings. Being aware of our actions and our words," Stella told Mags and Saz. They were seated around the fire pit in Stella's backyard late one afternoon. "It's like our moods and emotions move in cycles, like seasons and years. The trick is to remember to concentrate and focus on the positives, even when we are distracted by the ways of the world."

The Magic

L**una**

"I never thought we would be sitting at this bar with you, like the old days," Catherine looked at her friend as she polished the tankards.

"I am very glad that we are," Tizzie agreed.

"It will be time to open the tavern soon," Catherine hung the tankards along the back wall of the bar. "Tizzie has her dress shop. What are you going to do? I am sure we could both use help serving customers. If you got bored." All three crones laughed at that. It was good to be together again.

"It seems my old apothecary is empty and in need of some work. That's where you will find me." Luna felt younger and more energetic than she had in years. As tempting as it was to go back to see how Annie was going in the cottage, she promised herself she would immerse herself into life with her coven for the next six months and let Annie write her story. Her instinct told her to let things be for now. After all, if Annie had found her, maybe she would be reunited with Freddie, Lizzie and Katie as well.

In this realm, magic was growing. She had a feeling her skills would be needed someday soon. For the first time in a long time, she was looking forward to the future.

Stella

Magic was growing. Stella felt it all the time.

"I think it is because I believe in myself and I respect myself more. People treat me differently," she told Mags and Saz. They were sitting on the verandah out the back of Stella's house.

"In the last year, I have moved into my own home. I have a job that I enjoy most of the time. Two of my children are spending time with me. I will keep manifesting a world in which I am also in contact with Pedro and Kay. I have learnt that I have magical powers. I have travelled through portals. I have travelled overseas to Stonehenge. I have met some wonderful friends." Stella passed the tray of cupcakes to Saz and Mags.

"I would be crazy not to have changed how I think about myself. It sounds silly now, but I kind of did save the world." Even though she had shared her story with them, she still felt a little silly saying that out loud.

"When do you think we can go through the portal?" Saz asked quietly. "I don't mean to be impatient, but you have told us so much about it, I feel like I know the place already."

"We have probably visited there in a previous lifetime," Mags said.

"We will travel through for Beltane, which is soon." Stella shared her friend's excitement at the thought of traveling through with her friends.

"Have either of you had any luck with traveling in your dreams?" Stella knew they both dreamt of times past and of people from other lifetimes.

"I think I nearly did the other night," Mags replied. "I was in a forest with a coven. I think I was watching something important. But I woke up before I could work out what was happening."

"Tonight, if you want to, as you go to sleep, try to go back to that same place you saw in your dream. Remember as much about it as you can. You might be able to get back to where you were. Then you could try to interact with the people you saw, or at least get closer to hear what they are saying."

"If you don't mind, Stella, I have to say that I am not comfortable doing that. I mean, I know you can travel through dreams like that. It scares me and Saz. We will leave that to you. If you don't mind," Mags said.

"Please don't feel you have to take part in anything to do with magic or anything else that you don't want to," Stella said. "I want to share everything I know with you both. But you don't have to take part in anything that makes you feel uncomfortable."

"So, how about another cup of tea and some chocolates? I think I have some hidden in the back of the fridge." Stella walked over to the bench and turned on the kettle.

"Thanks, sis. You don't mind me calling you sis, do you? I feel like we are sisters." Saz smiled, taking the last cupcake, before taking the plate to the sink in the kitchen.

"I don't mind at all." Stella took the box of chocolates from the fridge and handed it to Saz. "Would you mind taking this to the table? I will bring out the cups when the kettle boils."

"HOW ABOUT WE MAKE SOME herb pouches this afternoon?" Mags was at the sewing machine when Stella returned with the teas. "We could play around with the different herbs you have growing in the pots out here."

"Sounds perfect." Stella raised her cup, "To us!"

Later that afternoon, Stella looked up from where she was planting her first row of lavender in her newly dug garden. She was sure she had heard footsteps, the tiniest footsteps as if Lexie or one of her friends was watching.

"Lexie, if you are there," Stella whispered loudly. "I am starting my medicinal herb garden at last! It has been a long year, but with so many things to be grateful for. I have a garden of my very own!"

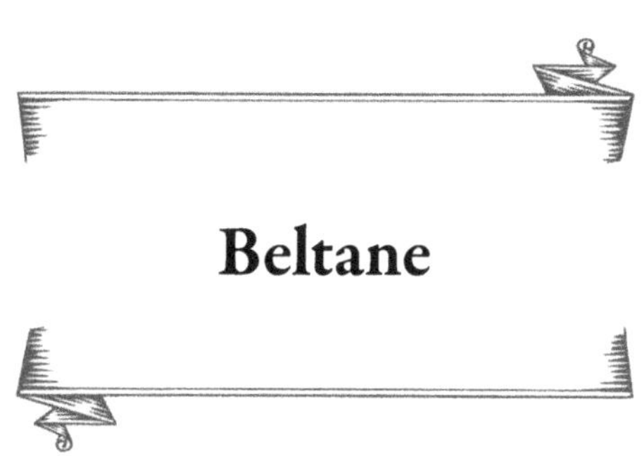

Beltane

Luna and Stella
Crone wisdom isn't something that can be gained from studying a book, even a grimoire or a book of spells. Stella and Luna both knew that. Wisdom was entwined with age and experience. Dramas, wars, trauma and disagreements were all part of life. The journey was made easier with family and friends.

In Australia, Beltane falls on October 31. It is the midpoint between spring and summer. A time to celebrate fertility, growth, and abundance and to honour the sacred union between the god and the goddess. This sabbat marks the beginning of summer and is associated with fertility, passion, and creativity. It is a time to celebrate the abundance of the earth and to honour the sacred union between the god and goddess. It is a time to connect with the energy of the sun and deepen our connection to the earth and the cycles of life and death.

Luna was always a little concerned about lighting fires in Australia in October, it could already be very warm, and everyone knows fires can easily get out of hand. Instead, she would light candles and incense and burn them in celebration of this day.

Broomhilda
The awakening was slow. Across the worlds, fairies, elves, sprite, magicians, those who practiced the craft of magic found evidence of it everywhere. In some cases, it was a subtle shift. In other realms, it was stronger. New varieties of flowers and plants with brighter colours than were ever seen before. New species of insects and birds, with shiny wings and shimmering feathers that shone and sent sparks into the atmosphere. Electric energy in the atmosphere was seen as sparks of colour, like little fireworks, randomly occurring in the forests, wood-

lands, and urban areas. People who hadn't identified as having magical skills were exhibiting increasing awareness and intuition.

Portals were opening again, linking the realms. Broomhilda was pleased that so far, this time, the portals weren't causing issues.

"I guess the increase in magic means there is no need for anyone to behave badly. Or is the flow of magic causing balance? An equilibrium across the realms," she wondered.

Changes were noticed in the realms where magic was unrecognized and where it had previously been illegal to practice magic. The council that met at The Fairy Glen were meeting regularly. They were slowly changing the way magic was perceived. It was still illegal in some places to use magic. The council had managed to change the penalty from prison, or worse, to community service, at least in most places.

"That no one has decided to start a war or stockpile magic is an amazing feat," the fairy told her group, gathered in their own fairy glen.

"We still need to keep an eye out for anything that looks suspicious."

Each fairy gathered and nodded in agreement. One of their biggest fears was that the strongest magicians would once again try to wipe out non-magical beings.

"This is a huge responsibility for us," Broomhilda continued. "But we know that our friends will continue to support us." For over four hundred years, the fairies, elves and sprites had successfully worked together across realms to support witches and wizards as well as ordinary people who had powers. They kept an eye out for any kind of malevolent activity. "Another advantage of the growth of magic across the realms is that it will be easier to keep in contact and pass information to each other when we need to."

The fairy was convinced that this was a beginning rather than an ending. Magic was not going to melt away for another twenty years. It would likely surge time and again. She knew she could rely on Luna, Stella, Logan and the others to help keep things under control. As always, she would keep her watchful eye over all the realms.

"I have the feeling that we are going to see a lot of new magic, new ideas and ways of manipulating the world around us." Everyone nodded in agreement.

Luna

Meeting Annie after so many years had changed Luna.

"I feel like I am years younger, I have more energy, I am more nimble, and my brain fog is clearing. I don't feel like I need to go back and spend time with Annie or even to find the others." Luna passed a tray of empty tankards and bowls to Catherine.

"I have always wanted to know what happened to my children. I thought they were lost forever. You know that's why I left so abruptly and hid away for so long." Her friends nodded.

"Then Annie found me, either accidentally or on purpose. I thought I would want to stay with her forever, to spend time with her and discover what happened and where her siblings are. But instead, I felt a confidence I have never felt before, that everything is going to fall into place," she confided to Tizzie and Catherine.

The witches were in Catherine's tavern. The tavern was bustling these days. With the growth of magic, people were moving more freely through the realms.

"The portals are open again, and people are behaving themselves. It is good to see business is booming." Catherine was in her element, as a bartender, as confidante to the nomadic bunch that loved her ales, pies and hearty stews. "I love the energy of the people in here."

Tizzie looked around at the men and women, laughing, talking and singing. "Magic is definitely good for business. Not only here, I am getting more customers at my shop, the markets are getting more popular, and Luna, your apothecary is getting a name for itself far and wide. That couple the other day had travelled for days to find you."

Luna nodded. "It feels like I had never left. I feel like a whole new person, the witch I was always meant to be. When I was here before, there was chaos, drama and wars. The tragedy that came after broke me. I hibernated." Luna bit her bottom lip as tears threatened. "Now I have contact with Annie, and it feels like maybe everything is going to work out. I am not saying that I won't go back and visit Annie before the six months is up. I am going to try my best not to stalk her or spy on her. I am going to trust that this time it will work out." Luna handed her tankard back to Catherine. "In the meantime, I'll be at my apothecary, taking inventory so we know which tinctures and infusions we have to make." Luna waved as she left the tavern. Her two friends exchanged glances, smiling at how things were working out.

Neither woman noticed the group of young people watching the crone leave the tavern.

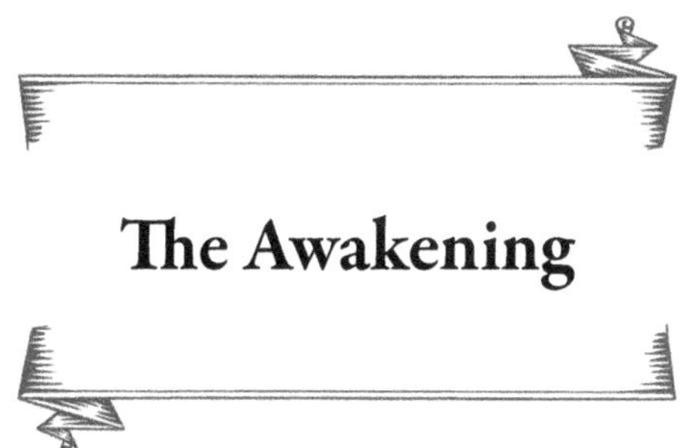

The Awakening

S tella

Stella noticed changes in her surroundings. Subtle changes in the weather. Plants growing more quickly. Flowers and fruits were bigger and brighter than before. All of nature was thriving as magic grew in strength, even in her world.

"It is like I am more attuned to nature and the world around me," she told Brigid and Maisie. She still visited her friends at least twice during the week. She preferred to travel through the portal in the back of her wardrobe. It was easier than travelling through her dreams. She was still always tired the next morning but with less of a hangover.

"I might be imagining it, but when I visit, everything feels more. More electric, more energy. More people," she said, looking around at the tavern full of people drinking and eating, celebrating life.

"We feel it too," Maisie replied. Brigid nodded her agreement. "Everything is more. Vivid. Electric. Magic. People are feeling more. Intuitively."

"We thought this might cause issues or fights," Brigid added. "So far, we haven't seen anything that causes concern. Logan is keeping an eye out across the realms, and the fairies and their teams are also keeping tabs on everything."

"You will let me know if there are any problems," Stella checked.

"Of course," Maisie replied. "How are Mags and Saz?"

Stella sighed a little. "They are not comfortable learning any more magic. They are both happy with how things are. It is disappointing. But I have you two as my coven, and then Mags and Saz are friends with whom I have a lot in common."

"We will teach you what we can," Brigid said as she gathered tankards up from the tables to refill them for the lively patrons. "I suspect soon you will be teaching us."

Stella blushed. "Thank you for the vote of confidence." She checked her phone, which she carried with her to keep track of the time. "I guess I should be getting back. I wish I could spend more time with you both, not just at night time. It would be so much fun."

"Why don't you?" Maisie asked as Stella was putting on her robes for her trip back home.

"Why don't I what?" Stella asked.

"Move here. Stay here with us. Start your own business. Learn more, practice magic all the time." Stella looked at Maisie for signs of a joke, but it seemed her friend was serious.

"I am being serious," Maisie confirmed.

"That sounds amazing," Stella admitted. "But I have my girls, my new home and work. I can't just leave all that behind."

"Maybe you could do what Luna is doing. Have someone look after your house and your pets for a few months?" Brigid suggested.

"Maybe," Stella conceded. "It certainly sounds tempting. Let me think about it." As Stella left her coven, she thought about Maisie's suggestion. The idea of spending more time with them was appealing.

Stella woke up to noises in her kitchen.

"Stay here," she whispered to Puddles as she quietly got out of bed. Wishing she had some kind of weapon, she slowly opened her bedroom door, ready for whatever was making a commotion in her kitchen.

"Surprise!" Andie and Emily embraced their mum with big smiles on their faces.

"We made you breakfast. Actually, we bought it from the bakery, but that's not the point." Andie said.

"Come and sit down," Emily said leading her to the dining room table.

"It's not my birthday, or Mother's Day or Christmas. What is the occasion?" Stella asked.

"Can't we just spoil you because you are our mother and we love you?" asked Andie with a mischievous smile on her face.

"Ah ha, well thank you both very much. You are amazing, and I love you." Stella picked up one of the dainty fairy cakes. "These look beautiful." She took a bite. "And they taste pretty good too."

Emily handed Stella a mug. "Mocha on oat milk. Special treat."

"Yum," agreed Stella. "So, what are you both up to this weekend?"

"Well," Andie began. "The thing is, we thought we would spend the day with you," she put her arm around her mum.

"I love that idea," Stella said. "Any thoughts on what we can do? Gardening maybe or cooking?" she teased her daughters, who weren't fans of her hippy witchy hobbies.

"It's getting warmer, so we thought we could take a lunch cruise on the lake. We were always going to do that, but we never get around to it," Emily suggested. "We brought our camera so we can take photos. We know you like it when we remember the photos."

"I do like photos of the time we spend together, of your beautiful smiling faces," she agreed.

"We can play with Puddles while you get ready," Emily scooped up the kitten as Andie picked up the ball of wool. Both girls loved Puddles and would happily spend hours playing with him.

Stella was ready in less than ten minutes. "I love that you decided to surprise me. Spending time with you both is my favourite way to spend the day." Stella ignored the glance exchanged between her daughters. They would tell her in their own time. For the moment, she was content to go with the flow. As they linked arms on their way out the door, she knew these times were too precious to move to the other realm, no matter how much she loved Maisie and Brigid. Her children would always come first.

"Yeah, about that. We do have some news. We were going to tell you after our lunch but now is as good a time. Promise you won't get mad or sad." Andie said.

"Oh dear," thought Stella. "I promise," she said. She sat down on the garden bench, beckoning for them to join her.

"You know how I have always wanted to travel overseas?" Emily started. Stella nodded.

"I applied for a job as a nanny in England, and I got the job! It means I can see the UK and parts of Europe. I will be away for at least six months. We thought maybe you could come and visit."

"That's amazing, Emily. Congratulations! Of course I will visit you. I will bring Andie too." Stella had no idea how she was going to do that, but it sounded amazing. She was so happy for Emily to be able to follow her dream of travelling. "That's exciting. I am pleased for you. I am not sad, I promise."

Andie replied, "Good. By the way, I am going too."

"Of course you are coming too. We will work it out and visit Emily together,"

"No, Mum I mean I am going with Emily. I can work there too. As a barista, probably, or as a waitress. Dad has already said yes, but he doesn't really want us to go."

"He even said if we went, he wouldn't visit us."

"One last thing, Mum," Emily continued, "We asked Kay or Pedro if they would come and visit you when we were overseas, but they said no. We are sorry."

Stella took a deep breath and looked at both of her beautiful children.

"I think you are both amazing young ladies. You have both decided what you want in life, and you have made plans to make it happen. You have been given an amazing opportunity. To travel overseas at your age. You will learn so much." She held back the tears that threatened to flow. One of the benefits of her magical powers was the ability to control her emotions and her body.

"I will miss you, but I will be okay. I will come and visit you. We can keep in touch on Skype and Facebook. I look forward to hearing all about your adventures."

"I AM TOUCHED THAT YOU thought of asking Kay and Pedro to look in on me. I will be fine. You have met Mags and Saz. Plus, I have Harry and Puddles, so I don't talk to myself anymore."

Stella stood up, putting her hands out to Andie and Emily. "So let's get going to that lunch cruise you promised me. I was thinking, on the way home, we could call into the plaza, and I could buy you some luggage for the trip, unless you already have some."

STELLA DIDN'T SEE THE letter at first.

She was preoccupied with waving until Emily's car disappeared around the corner. Four weeks until the girls travelled overseas. They had promised to have an early Christmas celebration before they left. Her head was spinning. She was so proud of them. So much change over the last twelve months. She wasn't the same person she was twelve months ago.

"I wonder if my increased confidence and my powers have had anything to do with the improvements in my life, in my circumstances and relationships," Stella mused as she picked the dead flowers from her geraniums, tucking them in the pot for compost.

"I am so grateful for all the opportunities and experiences." She thought, looking around at the beautiful haven she was creating.

STELLA WAS SUPPOSED to be catching up with Mags and Saz the next day, so she was surprised to see the letter in Mags' writing tucked into her screen door. She opened the envelope and read the note.

Stella,

We are so pleased we met you. You are an amazing person and will always be our friend. But if we are honest, the magic scares us. It was okay when it was on television or in books and we could pretend. When we learnt magic was real, we thought we could handle it, but we can't. We are really sorry, but we have to ask if we can have a break for a while. We know you will understand. We will always be your friends.

Forever. Mags and Saz.

Stella sat down on the purple sofa. "I don't know whether to laugh or cry." Puddles settled into her lap. "I don't feel like a cigarette or any wine, but a coffee would be great."

Stella heard the unmistakable sound of the kettle. She stood up, holding Puddles.

"It's only me." Stella recognized Lexie's voice immediately. "I heard you had a busy day and felt like a coffee, so I thought I would help,"

"Thank you," Stella replied. Could today get any stranger? She wondered.

"Probably," Lexie responded, reading her mind. "So what are you going to do?"

"About what?" Stella countered as she joined the sprite in the kitchen.

"WELL, WITH THE GIRLS moving overseas and that letter you just got, are you going to stay or go?"

"It is tempting to spend some time with Maisie and Brigid," Stella conceded. "But what about my job and my home and pets?"

"I'm sure you could figure that out if you wanted to. Good luck." Lexie hopped through the gap in the window Stella had left open to let fresh air in while they were out.

Stirring her coffee, Stella thought back over her day.

"Twelve months ago, I would have been heartbroken if the girls had told me they were planning to move overseas. Now I am excited about the opportunities they have and that I can visit them," she told Puddles. "We have grown so much closer this year, and I am so grateful for that."

"I would have been devastated receiving that note from Mags and Saz. Now I am pleased that I met those two lovely ladies. I understand their desire to feel safe and normal." She let Puddles sit on the bench, something she wouldn't normally do. It was that kind of day.

"It is sad that the other two aren't ready to visit me, yet. I am sure that will change soon enough," She mused. "Magic doesn't necessarily mean happy endings, at least not always in the way we expect it to.

"So the question that remains is, what am I going to do now?"

The end is but the beginning, in a circular world full of cycles and seasons.

We learn, we teach, we seek knowledge and truth,

We grow, we challenge, we change,

We love, we laugh, we live life to the fullest,

We give thanks for the very being of our existence and of those before us and those yet to come,

We are but a very small part in a very big world,

But we mean the world to some, and they mean the world to us.

The circle of life, and the seasons, everything in its place

As it should be – So mote it be

The End

www.ingramcontent.com/pod-product-compliance
Lightning Source LLC
Chambersburg PA
CBHW061102100726
47911CB00012B/346